L.A. SLEEPERS

L.A. SLEEPERS

A Hollywood Ghostwriter Mystery

DAKOTA DONOVAN

SUGAR SKULL PRESS
LOS ANGELES, CALIFORNIA

Published by Sugar Skull Press, Los Angeles

ISBN-13: 978-0692201121

ISBN-10: 0692201122

Cover photo from the Everett Collection, used by permission.

Sugar Skull Press publishes classic and contemporary crime
novels as well as classic and gothic mysteries.

For available titles, please visit our website: sugarskullpress.com.

Please direct inquiries to sugarskullpress@gmail.com or contact us at:

Sugar Skull Press
P.O. Box 292357
Los Angeles, CA 90029

For M,
who asked for the story and was first to read it.

"It seemed like a nice neighborhood to have bad habits in."

RAYMOND CHANDLER, *The Big Sleep*

◀ ONE ▶

When my cell phone rings, I'm soaking in the bathtub, puffing on an electronic cigarette, and rereading *The Big Sleep*. The last thing I want to do is answer an unexpected call.

I'm behind on my rent, overdue on my credit card payments, still owe my dentist for a root canal, and about to have the electricity turned off. If the phone is ringing, and the fricking thing rings night and day, it's somebody who wants money—money I don't have.

But I have to answer—the person on the other end might want to hire me for a writing gig.

On the fifth ring of the ringtone—the opening bars of Bach's "Sleepers Awake"—I grab my cell from the shelf next to the tub and answer the way I always answer.

"Boo! It's Dakota Donovan."

"I'm looking for a ghostwriter," the man says. He has the quavering voice of someone in his eighties.

"Memoir?"

"Y-e-s," he answers, turning the short word into three syllables. "I need you to start right away."

I know what's coming.

" . . . I'm dying."

▼

It's a Brentwood address, so I take Sunset from my place in Hollywood—I no longer trust my 1998 Toyota to the freeways. The route is definitely the long way around—through tourist traps, the Sunset Strip, UCLA, twisting and turning and curving up and away.

After I find the address, I drive about a block past it and walk back—the better not to be seen in an old car, my dear. Anyway, I can always use a good walk. All the hours sitting in front of a computer are working unwonders on my forty-something backside. Not that I tell anybody my age—I hide it the way I try to hide my car. And it isn't easy sans Botox,

9

plastic surgery, or the money for gym memberships, spas, personal trainers, facials—or even a good haircut.

As I make my way up the Brentwood street that yawns the heavy breath of most overgrown behemoths—overfed, overwatered, overpleasured, overmedicated, overcompensated—I wonder about the people who live in these multimillion dollar homes. What are their stories? How did they get here? How do they stay here? Will Client A (if he gives me the job and lives that long) refer other Brentwoodites with stories to tell?

What a joke. If there's one thing a ghostwriter never gets, it's referrals—even if the book is a bank-account-bloating success. The "authors" I work with always take credit for the books—and even come to believe they've written them. As a ghostwriter, I'm very good—and this proves it.

The house is a fine midcentury load of bricks—the type of house I adore, the house I'd pick for myself: not too large, not too small, more than just right.

But instead of feeling envious, I'm curious—and happy I can get a look inside the place. Who knows when I'll need to use it as a setting for one of my books—my own books, the novels I write under my own name, when I have time to write them. But, hell, if other writers, better writers, famous writers—F. Scott Fitzgerald, for one—were broke most of the time and had to scramble to survive, why should I be exempt?

When I reach the destination, I take a deep breath, straighten my sunglasses, force a smile, and get ready to meet the author.

Before I have a chance to knock, the door flings open and a short, slight man, probably in his early eighties, stands in the open doorway. A fedora sits at a jaunty angle on his head, and he's dressed in a well-pressed double-breasted gray suit, white shirt, and striped blue tie. He appears to be on his way out, and I wonder if I have the wrong address. But I know it's the right place when the man steps aside so I can enter, while staring at me through cloudy cataracts.

Without speaking, I take off my sunglasses, then face the man for what seems like a long time. My initial encounter with an author is a significant moment—an animal-like sizing up each other. I know if the prospective client hires me, I'll become a combination confessor, psychiatrist, minister, sister, friend, enemy—someone who learns the person's deepest, darkest secrets, or probes until the client reveals them, and it will be a wild ride, as the author loves, hates, resents, despises, and finally appreciates me. Both author and writer just have to hang on until the book is finished. This is my main advantage over other ghostwriters—I can make it through all the crazy stages and end up with a completed book. I have a high tolerance for confrontation.

"Good afternoon," the man says. On the phone he'd told me his name was Milton. In person, he looks like a Milton—and sounds like one, with a deep, well-modulated voice, without any trace of the shakiness he'd displayed on the phone. It's hard to believe I'm speaking with the same person.

"Hello," I say, as I walk through the door.

When I step inside, I have the sense that I've been in this house before, and feel an espresso shot of déjà vu.

As I stare at the rear wall—floor-to-ceiling glass—it occurs to me where I've seen Milton's house—a *Columbo* rerun on Netflix, when I could still afford the service.

Ghostwriting Rule #1: *Find a point of conversation and get the client talking.*

"What a beautiful home," I remark. "It would make a wonderful movie location."

I turn to smile at Milton—hoping he'll mention that the house has appeared in a TV show. Instead, he removes his fedora and tosses it toward a hat rack on the wall, where—bull's-eye!—it lands on the center peg surrounded by other fedoras (or is it "fedori"?). Either the old man's eyesight isn't that bad or he's had a lot of ring toss practice.

I need to get him talking.

"Have you lived here long?"

"Built the place," he answers. "Pioneer days."

"Back when? The fifties?"

"Those were the days," he says. "The really, really good old days."

" . . . and you want to write about them," I say, smiling in understanding.

"Hell, no," Milton replies in a voice that sounds too big for his small body.

"I'm looking forward to learning what you have in mind for the book," I say, trying to smooth over this first bump in the ghostwriting road. It's never a good sign when a prospective client's answer starts with the word "hell."

I really, really want, and really, really need this job. Judging by Milton's surroundings, he should be able to afford my full rate—twenty thousand for a book, completed in four months. It isn't a fortune, but it's enough to live on—almost.

"Follow me to my study," he instructs, leading me at a fast pace through bright, high-ceilinged rooms, where the furniture is pristine Midcentury Modern—gorgeous, to-die-for tables, desks, chairs, lamps, sofas, and credenzas.

I worship Danish Modern the way some people idolize other great Nordic-related art—Hamlet, Beowulf, and the works of Hans Christian Andersen and Isak Dinesen. The place is a Midcentury Modern museum—with collector's items worth hundreds of thousands of dollars. I'm thrilled just to breathe the same atmosphere as the glorious furniture.

But when Milton turns a corner and leads me into his study, the room isn't decked out in sleek midcentury furnishings. It's a dusty, musty, fusty home office with a scratched-up metal desk, floor-to-ceiling filing cabinets, and lots of wires every-where. The entire vibe is anti-creative, dank, and stale.

"Have a seat," Milton croons, as if ushering me to a table at a classic Hollywood nightclub—the Cocoanut Grove or Ciro's.

I start to sit on a rickety folding chair, but Milton grabs my elbow and pushes me toward the low-slung, dingy beige couch.

"Make yourself comfortable," he tells me.

I sink into the close-to-the-ground discomfort of the monstrosity couch—feeling as if my knees are going to hit my chin every time I move my head. I'm glad, so glad, I'm wearing slacks.

Milton removes his suit jacket and drapes it over the back of his desk chair. Then he settles into the chair, which is raised so high that the old man's feet don't quite touch the ground. He crosses his legs and one foot keeps kicking in my direction. I figure he is either trying to send me a message—"I'm in charge here"—or the action proves that restless leg syndrome does, in fact, exist.

"So . . ." I begin, hooking my hands over one knee and taking a deep breath.

"So, what are you going to charge me?" Milton says, peering down at me from his swivel-chair throne.

"Could you tell me a bit more about what you'd like to do?"

"I want to put it all down on paper," Milton replies. "Like I told you on the phone."

All Milton had mentioned during the phone call was that he was dying and wanted to finish a book, "A-SAP."

"Your life story? A novel? Something work-related? I'm not sure what you're looking for," I say in my lowest, most well-modulated tones. Put the client at ease. Make the author feel comfortable.

"It's better for you," Milton replies, "if I don't say whether it's fact or fiction."

In the blip before saying anything, I try to figure out why it's "better" for me not to know whether Milton's story is fact or fiction. Better for my safety? (Does he want to write about the mob?) Better for my writing? (Does he not want to bind me with the facts?) Better for my peace of mind? (Is he going to admit to crimes?)

"I hear you," is my noncommittal response.

"We'd need to finish in about eight weeks," he says, giving me a grim, close-mouthed grin.

Eight weeks is pushing it for a book—but if we start right away and if he pays me enough so I can focus only on his project, and I work twelve-plus hours a day, I can probably pull it off. It isn't the writing that takes time—I write fast—it's gathering the facts for the story. Some people meander all over the place before they come up with even one usable anecdote.

"Well, we'd need to get started right away," I say, glad for a legitimate reason to give Milton a nudge.

"So what's this going to set me back?"

"My usual rate is twenty thousand, but since this is a rush project..."

"I'll pay you four grand, flat," he states, leaning back and folding his arms over his starched shirtfront.

Four thousand! Lord, the Rougier lamp in his living room is worth more than that! I know that if I take the job for such a paltry fee I'll regret it. I'll kill myself to finish the book—since I can't lower my standards, and will deliver the same quality of work whatever the client pays me. I'll have to take on side jobs just to get by.

But I don't hesitate with my answer.

"All right," I say. "Let's get started."

◀ TWO ▶

I watch as Milton navigates his swivel chair to the metal filing cabinet against the wall, opens a drawer, and removes a large ledger checkbook. He rolls back toward me and sits with the black spiral binder on his lap. After flipping open the checkbook, he stares for a moment in my direction, where I sit like a hunched crab on the low-to-the-floor couch.

I take a deep breath as Milton grabs a pen from his desk. I know what this means. He's going to give me a deposit! It's a real job!

"How do you spell your name?" the old man asks.

"Dakota, like the state."

"There's no state called Dakota."

"D-A-K . . ." I begin.

"Not so fast," he says, holding his filmy eyes close to the lime-green check.

I wonder how much Milton intends to put down. I usually ask for twenty-five percent—but we haven't even reached the point of me giving him a contract. Well, I'm not about to turn down any money. Even a check for a hundred bucks would help at this point.

"D-A-K . . ." Milton repeats, then says, "go on."

After ten minutes, my name is at last on Milton's check. While he makes out the rest of it, I glance around the room, as if interested in all the clutter and detritus. I don't want to stare and appear too anxious for the money.

Finally I hear the welcome sound of a check ripped away on the perforated line. When I turn my head toward him, Milton has the check raised high in the air, with his hand extended toward me, as if asking a dog to sit for a bone.

Instead of taking it from him, I lift my palm. He moves the check toward me by degrees, and when it finally reaches me feels like a rare bird quivering in my hand.

I decide not to look at the amount. Whatever it is, I'll take it.

I pick up my bag, open the flap, and as I start to place the check in a zipper compartment, spot the amount: $4,000.

I look up at Milton, tempted to say something, but decide against it. Why get into a discussion that might lead to no check at all?

Milton seems to know what I'm thinking.

"I've got my reasons for paying you upfront," he says. "But don't get any ideas about taking my money and running. I know people . . ."

Before I can respond, Milton swivels around, pulls open a desk drawer, and with two hands removes a brown legal-sized accordion file stuffed with papers in varying alignments and colors. He heaves the file toward me, and I grab it from him.

"I want you to take that with you and review the contents," Milton says, pointing at the file on my lap.

Milton rolls his chair closer to me, leans down, pats the folder, and whispers: "This is for your eyes only."

I have to resist the urge to laugh at Milton's earnest delivery —as if he's a spymaster sharing top secrets with an operative. But I tighten my lips, take a breath, and say, "I'd be happy to sign a confidentiality agreement if that would make you feel more comfortable."

Milton shakes his head. "Not necessary," he says. "Like I told you, if you try to double-cross me, I'll have you taken care of."

Despite my urgent need for money, I'm tempted to stuff the $4,000 check into Milton's liver-spotted hand, toss the accordion file at him, and sprint out of the place. If Milton is delusional, it will be next to impossible to complete the job. If Milton is speaking the truth, I don't need this kind of pressure or these types of threats. I'm just a fricking ghostwriter trying to help somebody tell his story before he dies.

"Milton," I say, "I'm starting to feel uncomfortable about this."

"Not trying to worry you."

"What's this all about?"

"I've been holding back this story for over thirty years, afraid to tell it. Everybody else involved died under mysterious circumstances. But I'm not going to live much longer, so I've decided to tell my tale."

"Don't you think I'll be in danger if you share the story with me?"

"You're a ghostwriter, aren't you?"

"Still," I tell him, "if the people you intend to write about are that dangerous, they're bound to find out I worked on the book."

"Nobody's going to find out. Like I said, all of this is for your eyes—and ears—only."

I sit in silence, trying to decide whether to keep going or get the hell out of here. Milton senses my hesitation.

"Tell you what," Milton says. "If you finish the book in even one day under eight weeks, I'll give you a two-thousand-dollar bonus."

I turn to the big black ledger checkbook on Milton's desk and picture him writing the $2,000 bonus check. I hold the accordion folder close to my body and wrap my arms around it.

"Go home and read the file," Milton says, "then come back at the same time on Tuesday and we'll talk."

▼

It's 4:30 in the afternoon when I leave Milton's house with the accordion folder in a reusable shopping bag from Ralphs supermarket—Milton's way of camouflaging the material.

After Milton slams the front door behind me, I rush toward my car and have to resist looking over my shoulder to see if anyone is following me.

Even without checking for counterspies, the walk to my car seems ominous and endless on this August afternoon when no birds sing, no breezes blow, and the sun beats down on my unprotected hair and skin. I feel exposed, vulnerable, and just want to run home, flip on the air conditioning, and hide out in my darkened living room with a vat of iced tea or maybe something stronger.

Yes, I need to get home and read the "for your eyes only" file. Curiosity beckons, enticing me to learn more, more, more about the mysterious Milton—his background, his life, his activities, his reason for stifling his story for over thirty years.

But first things first. I need to reach the bank—on the clogged streets in the Friday rush—before it closes at six p.m. and deposit that check!

When I get to my car, I open the trunk and place the accordion folder inside a laundry basket and cover it with a bag of library books I need to return. Before closing the trunk, I have the feeling I've been through all this before, have done all this before, and have come to regret it. Most of all, I have the impression that I'm opening Pandora's box.

I turn and look toward Milton's house. This is the point when I can change my mind—before putting the author's check in the bank. If I deposit the check, I have only myself to blame if the job turns out to be a nightmare. I have a choice—I have a choice right now. I know the decision is up to me.

I jump in my car and drive straight to the bank.

◀ THREE ▶

I wake up to incoherent babbling outside my bedroom window. If a voice can resemble a ribbon of jagged glass with a buzzing undertone, this one fits the description. The sound seems to go on and on and on without the speaker pausing for breath. I often wake up to this noise that's like a groaning Greek chorus, the Earth itself vocalizing all the trouble it has seen.

As the voice spirals along, spinning tales no one can understand, yet that everyone within earshot on some level understands, I put my arm over my forehead, close my eyes, and think "Shut up!" I have a stabbing migraine, and would like to stay in bed for a while to see if it passes, but the babbler is only making the pain worse.

I place my palm on the left side of my head and press, stand up, and make my way to the bathroom and find the only medication that works during a migraine attack—Excedrin. After downing two tablets, I tie a cold, wet towel around my forehead. Now for the next two remedies—an ice pack and a cup of coffee.

▼

It's late Saturday morning when I sit on the living room floor and at last open the Milton Kingman file. In it, I find plastic sleeves filled with photos, patent applications, a range of documents (letters, memos, notes), and what looks like a laboratory diary in a spiral binder. Damn, I think, these are all originals—the photos, the notebook, the documents. I don't accept originals!

Not long after I moved to L.A., I was on the Metro Blue Line when a teenager took off running after grabbing my shoulder bag, which was full of original documents—priceless photos, handwritten letters, a diary, and more—research materials for a memoir I was ghostwriting for a socialite who wanted to tell the story of her years as a celebrated opera star.

The fallout had been horrific—the diva had fired me, demanded the return of her money, and had threatened to sue for negligence. What in the hell was I doing transporting such valuable material on a subway?

I was lucky to have survived the disaster—and vowed to never, ever, ever allow a client to give me original materials again. Ever.

What's wrong with me? Why didn't I check Milton's file before taking it with me? I know why. I was so desperate for a paying job, any paying job, that I'd blanked out, didn't even think about what the folder might contain.

I need to photocopy everything in Milton's file, and should go right to Kinkos—migraine or not—but think: *What if the documents get jammed in the machine? What if I leave something behind? What if someone sees what I'm copying? And what about the time and the cost?*

▼

When I wake up with my head on my laptop, it's light outside and for a moment I wonder if it's the following day. My head still throbs. I'd fallen asleep while categorizing the contents of Milton's folder—which features patent applications for a variety of arcane inventions, including a water battery that never runs out of energy.

I jump up and rush to Desk #2, where the digital clock marks the passage of time in days, hours, minutes, and seconds. The timepiece—a gift from my daughter, and one of the most useful presents I've ever received—is a central figure in my existence. I rely on the Seiko R-Wave atomic clock to lead me, guide me, tell me what the hell time it is.

I blame my missing sense of time on my Irish blood. I can lose hours in what seems like seconds, and sometimes seconds seem like hours. My missing sense of time—the Dakota Donovan Time Warp—is a curse when it comes to functioning in the real world, making a living, running a business, and showing up on time for appointments.

But my screwed-up sense of time is much, much worse when I have a migraine. Sometimes I spend what seems like eons climbing an endless Escher staircase, and there's nothing I can do except try reach the end of it.

My ringtone sends out the first bars of Bach's "Sleepers Awake," and I stumble around holding my hand over my left temple, trying to push the pain away, as I search the apartment. When I locate the phone on Desk #1, I note the caller ID: Private Number. I usually let these calls go to voicemail—because it might be a creditor or my dentist's collection agency. But there's just a chance that someone is calling about a job. And if I'm going to survive for the next few months, I need to supplement my income.

"Boo! It's Dakota Donovan," I answer, using my running ghostwriter joke.

Before he even says a word, I know who it is, just by his sharp intake of breath. I can also tell from the brief sound that the person is anxious, perhaps even a trifle annoyed. How can I detect so much from such a small clue? Because I'm a ghostwriter and spend hundreds of hours each year talking to people about their lives. If I can't read people by now, I should find a new line of work.

I wait, but the person doesn't say anything. Before I can repeat my usual greeting, I hear an exhale that sounds like a man blowing through a straw to test his lung capacity.

Breathing, in and out. Inhale. Exhale. This is how human beings mark time—and it's far more accurate that a Seiko R-Wave Atomic Clock.

Another deep inhale, then a slow exhale, then: "I see you deposited my check."

I try to figure out why Milton is calling about this. He'd offered to pay for his ghostwriting project in advance. Did he expect me to hold onto the check until I complete the assignment?

I collapse onto the bare floor of the living room, and press my forehead against my knee trying to constrict the dilated blood vessels of my raging headache.

"Wasn't I supposed to deposit it?"

"How's the job coming along?"

"I'm reading through the file, cataloging the material, and preparing my questions and comments. I'll be ready when we meet on Tuesday," I say to reassure him.

"Let's meet tomorrow," Milton says.

"I really need more time to study the file."

"Come over and we'll go over everything together."

"I have commitments tomorrow."

"If you're not going to be cooperative, I'll find somebody who will be."

"I need at least another day to study the file, Mr. Kingman."

"Call me Milton."

"Milton, to do a good job, I need time to review what's in the folder."

"Come over tomorrow at two p.m. or the deal is off."

"I have appointments," I say.

"On a Sunday?"

"Yes."

"Reschedule them."

"I really can't do that."

"Then give me my money back. I'll find somebody else."

"We made a deal and set a time, Milton. Let's just keep to that."

"I need to work with somebody who's flexible."

"Milton, we need to make a schedule and stick to it. We both have lives."

As soon as I tell him this, I know it's the wrong thing to say. If he's dying, as he'd told me the first day, Milton has very little time left. He probably doesn't focus on the mundane details of his life—for him, it's all the big stuff. And the book is at the top of the list. Okay, all right. But I can't meet any time of any day, whenever he calls. I have things to do!

"I'm sorry, Milton, but I can't meet tomorrow."

"Then I want my money back. And if you try to screw me, I know people who can set you straight."

◀ FOUR ▶

I have to talk myself into going to the Sunday meeting with Milton—because it's counter to everything I believe about working with clients. If you let the authors start to push you around or feel as if they own all your time—which most of them do—you'll have no life left. They'll call at all hours— making demands, insisting on impromptu interviews at three in the morning, requiring last-minute in-person meetings way the hell across town.

But here I am driving from Hollywood to Brentwood at 12:45 p.m. in my gas-guzzler (the car is long overdue for a tune-up). The trip back and forth will eat up twenty bucks in fuel. At this rate, after eight weeks of working on Milton's book, I'll drive away much of my fee.

After a seventy-five-minute winding drive down Sunset, I park my car on an old-money Brentwood street. As I walk up Milton's block, I feel the Sunday afternoon lull wash over me like a warm waterfall. The temperature is a tolerable eighty-five degrees, with a hint of a breeze tickling the lush, well-watered grass. All is quiet on the Brentwood front, and I assume it's because the people who occupy the houses moved in twenty or fifty plus years before—with kids grown and gone away. I enjoy quiet, but this seems almost too still, as if someone has vacuumed away all noise.

I'm transporting the confidential file in the same Ralph's shopping bag Milton gave me on Friday. Besides, I don't want the author to think I'm making enough money for fancy leather carrying cases.

When I'm within a few houses of my destination, Milton's door flings open and my elderly client jumps onto the front steps. He looks around and spots me—then begins to shake his head back and forth and hold up his hands as if to say, "Go back."

I don't know what Milton means, so I move toward him. Again, he thrusts his hands back and forth in a pushing motion. Why would he call me here, I ask myself, if he intends to send me right home? Maybe he has some kind of tic—restless arm syndrome—or maybe he suffers from St. Vitus Dance.

Now Milton is shaking his head back and forth and pushing his hands forward and back, almost as if enacting a ritualistic dance or performing a head-banging at an AC/DC concert—I'd attended one for a writing assignment. For someone in his eighties, Milton has some moves.

From inside Milton's house, a man calls out in a whiny, nasal voice, "Daaadddddd! Daaaadddddd!"

Milton's head tilts toward the voice, then he turns back to me. The old man raises his right arm, moves his hand toward his face, extends his index finger and puts it to his lips. It is clear that he's telling me to "shhhh."

"Daaaddddd! Daaaaaaddddd!" whimpers a man from inside the house.

I don't know if I should stay or go—I've just spent over an hour driving to this Sunday afternoon appointment, and will spend over an hour driving home. I'm beyond annoyed at this waste of time—especially since I'm under such a tight deadline to complete Milton's book.

The owner of the whining voice crowds through the front door and stands there for a moment, giving me a chance to take in the scene. It's hard to believe this huge man is the diminutive Milton's son—and right away I wonder if he's adopted.

Around my age, mid-to-late-forties, the man is about 6'4" and weighs close to three hundred pounds. He is overdressed for the warm weather in a pullover sweater, jeans, and boots—as if he is on his way for a hike in the mountains.

The man reaches down, puts his hands on Milton's shoulders and starts to pull. "Get back in the house, Dad," he intones. "Get inside!"

Milton does a knee bend and dips out of his son's grip. I'm amazed at the old guy's agility. Milton spins around and raises his head so he's looking into his adversary's eyes.

"Get the hell out of here, Conrad. Vamoose!"

"You need somebody to take care of you," Conrad says in a tone that is neither caring nor comforting.

"If I need somebody, I'll hire somebody," Milton shoots back.

"Get in the house, Dad."

"No, you get out of my house. Leave me alone."

Conrad turns and stares at me, as if detecting my presence for the first time.

"What the hell do you want?"

I glance at Milton, who offers an almost imperceptible headshake to indicate I'm not to give anything away. For some reason, he doesn't want his son to know about the ghostwriting project. I figure the son doesn't want the father to spend any of his inheritance.

"Well . . ." Conrad adds, taking a step toward me.

"I'm just out for a walk," I counter.

Conrad shakes his head. "You don't live around here."

"I'm visiting a friend."

"Who?"

The hulking Conrad is now standing outside the front gate staring down at me. I'm 5'6"—but feel like a cartoon mouse next to this gargantuan.

"Go home, Conrad," Milton yells from the porch. "Get in your car and get the hell out of here."

Conrad turns, and utters in a deep whine, "I'm moving in."

Before Milton can respond, a blue pony runs out of the front door—or at least I think that's what it is. The creature scuttles around Conrad and nearly knocks over Milton before racing down the front walk, making a right turn, and heading for the Santa Monica Mountains.

"Rudy! Rudy!" Conrad calls, rushing after the blue flash. "Come back here! Come back."

I turn and watch as Conrad does his best to hoof it after Rudy—whatever he is.

"Come on," Milton tells me. "Let's go inside. They won't be back for a while."

As Milton leads me through his bright, beautiful Brentwood home, I remark that I've never seen a more stunning collection of Midcentury Modern furniture, even in a magazine. But Milton doesn't respond. Instead, he remarks, "What did I ever do to deserve a son like that?"

"So you don't want Conrad to know you're writing a book."

"I don't want him sticking his nose where it doesn't belong," Milton replies. "Ever since I turned eighty, my son thinks he can take over my life, my money, and my business."

Before stepping into his office, Milton turns to me and says, "It's been worse lately. Conrad got laid off from his job and his wife is divorcing him. He has a lot of time on his hands to cause trouble for me. The worst is when he shows up unannounced, like he did today."

Milton steps aside and allows me to enter the office. I take out my tape recorder and set it on his desk, then grab my notebook and pen.

"How much time before Conrad gets back?" I ask, sitting on a metal folding chair and placing the Ralph's shopping bag with the confidential file at my feet.

"They should be gone for a long time," Milton says. "That dog can run about thirty miles an hour."

"Oh, so it was a dog."

"Conrad is president of the Great Dane Society of Greater Los Angeles."

"What was his day job before he got laid off?"

"He was working as a camera operator for one of the local news shows."

Milton takes his suit jacket from the back of his chair and puts it on, then removes a Panama hat from a peg on the wall and places it on his head. He picks up a cigar and a glass of what looks like Scotch and sits down.

The author gets right to the point—sketching out his story with broad strokes. He was a secret partner of billionaire tycoon Duke Galveston—movie mogul, entrepreneur, government defense contractor. Together, they developed a number of inventions that had the potential to change the balance of power in the world.

I hate to stop Milton's monologue, but need him to clear up something.

"Why did Duke Galveston pick you when he had hundreds of scientists in his defense businesses?"

"I produced some movies for him, and he decided he could trust me."

Milton sets his glass on the desk, sticks his unlit cigar in an ashtray, puts his hands behind his head, leans back in his chair, and raises his eyes toward the ceiling—going back in his mind, trying to remember.

"This started after the war, back in the forties and went on until Duke moved to Vegas in '66."

"Did you have any scientific or engineering training?" I ask.

"Duke and I were both self-taught. Anyway, we were able to reverse engineer everything that came from the aliens."

"Aliens?"

"I thought you read what was in the file I gave you," Milton says. "What in the hell have you been doing since Friday?"

As Milton spins his story—emphasizing that everyone who knew about the "alien" inventions, including Duke Galveston, had died under mysterious circumstances—I take notes and say to myself, "Oh, one of these."

Since moving to California, I've attracted an assortment of lunatic-fringe projects—from alien contactees to angel mediums, not to mention time travelers and psychic healers—so Milton's story doesn't shock or even surprise me. I've seen and heard some of the wildest tales imaginable—and pride myself on giving everyone my full attention and never bursting into derisive laughter. As long as nobody gets hurt and nothing is illegal, a paying customer is a paying customer—that is, a paying author.

I stare at Milton and say, "But this has already been written about." Since I've dealt so often with far-out types, I'm familiar with the canon.

When Milton doesn't respond, I continue, "The book was called *The Day After Roswell*. It was written by a retired

Army colonel, who claimed the Army reverse engineered what remained of the alien ship that crashed in Roswell, New Mexico, in 1947. The author was in charge of the project, which resulted in inventions such as lasers, integrated circuits, and fiber optics."

"Is that the book that came out in the late 1990s?" Milton asks.

"Right."

"Well, there's one big difference in what I'm telling you," Milton says and waits for me to respond.

"And what's that?" I ask, but—call it my ghostwriter's sixth sense—know what he's going to say.

"The difference is that we worked directly with the aliens."

And, I think, so do I—especially right now. But I don't let the old man know what's in my mind. I dive right in.

"So what's the story you want to tell, Milton?"

"Haven't you been listening?"

"What point do you want to make with your story?"

"I don't follow you."

"Is it a government-conspiracy story? Aliens-exist story? Celebrity-tell-all? Poor-boy-makes-good story? Suppressed-technology story?"

"A little of all that."

"But what's the major reason you want to write this book?"

"I'm going to die. I want to leave something big behind."

Well, there's always your gigantic son, I think, wondering when Conrad will return with his Great Dane. But that's not what I say.

"So when are we going to do the interviews?"

"What interviews?"

"I need to interview you to get the details on your story."

"I've told you what I remember. The rest is in the folder. I want a sixty-thousand-word manuscript in eight weeks. That's eight weeks from last Friday."

In a way, I'm relieved. I won't have to drive across town for interviews—saving time and gas money. The story is, according to Milton, all in the folder. And if there isn't enough to go on? Over the years, I've learned how to fill in the blanks—either through research, intuition, or imagination. I am, after all, a novelist.

Milton jumps up and grabs two slats in the window blinds, pulling them apart. He peers out the window as if he's a ship's captain espying the ocean waves.

"Quick," he commands, "they're coming back. Get in the closet."

◀ FIVE ▶

"Pardon me?"

"Get in the closet. Please," Milton says. "I don't want Conrad to see you here."

In the eye-blink of time I spend absorbing what Milton's words, I recall a play I'd once acted in—*A Flea in Her Ear* by Georges Feydeau. Yes, life imitates art—not the other way around—I'm now living a French farce.

" . . . and take your things with you," Milton says, pushing my tape recorder at me as I grab the Ralph's shopping bag that holds the confidential material.

I hear the front door yawn open and, before I know it, find myself crowding into a closet jammed with junk.

"Daaaddd! Daaaddd!" calls out Milton's son, in the sniveling voice of a spoiled manchild.

I hear Conrad's heavy boots pounding against the floors in the living room, then the sound of a dog's nails scratching against the hardwood.

Uh-oh, I think. The Great Dane is bound to come rushing up to this closet. How am I going to explain myself?

But Milton seems to have it under control. He jumps up, slams the door to his office, and starts yelling.

I try to make out his muffled speech, and, while I can't distinguish the words, the meaning comes across with no need for interpretation.

After a few exchanges between the two men, the front door slams, a car engine fires up, and the vehicle squeals away. I wonder if it's safe to leave the closet or if I'm supposed to wait for Milton to give me the all clear.

While I wait, I check out my surroundings. I fish around in my purse until I feel the cold metal of my penlight. With a click, the cramped closet is lit up, the tiny flashlight sending out white beams. Nothing interesting on my left—just boxes marked "taxes" and others marked "records." I turn and aim at the other side and see a pile of what looks like photo albums.

I don't hear any noise in the house, but think it best to wait a few minutes before venturing out of the closet. In the meantime, I decide to check out some photos.

I pull an album from the middle of the stack, set it on my lap, and flip to a random page. And there they are—Milton, with celebrated billionaire Duke Galveston towering over him at his famous 6'6". Both men face a small silvery being standing on a stainless steel table. The being, creature, entity, whatever the proper designation, seems to be holding forth, instructing and enlightening the two men on the ways and means of the universe.

I hope the photograph is a still from one of the low-budget sci-fi movies Milton and Galveston made during the 1950s. I really hope that's it.

The photo makes my heart palpitate in fright, but that doesn't prevent my curiosity from kicking in. I flip to another page and see a photo that depicts three of the silvery beings with an oval-shaped apparatus in front of them. Is this one of the alien inventions that Milton was talking about?

I put the album in my bag, click off my penlight, stand up, and put my hand on the closet doorknob. When I push open the door, it creaks—and I have the feeling I shouldn't make any noise. But why not? Milton's son and his canine pony are gone, aren't they?

What time is it anyway? I arrived at two p.m. So what time is it now? Time challenged as I am, I have no idea how long I've been in the closet looking at the photo album or how much time I spent talking to Milton before Conrad and Scooby-Doo returned.

I stand in Milton's office for a few moments glancing around. Something is missing. I scan the room from one end to the other and realize it's the filing cabinet—the one with the ledger checkbook and who knows what else. Did junior put it in storage? Did he appropriate the contents for himself?

When I step into the living room, I forget for a moment where I am. I'm transported to Midcentury Modern heaven. What a room! And, yes, I really believe that heaven will be outfitted in Danish Modern—from God's throne on down.

I don't see Milton in the living room or dining room and wonder if he's in the backyard—which I've never seen. So why not have a look—especially now that I have a good excuse: I'm looking for Milton.

As I enter the kitchen—with its celestial array of aqua blue vintage appliances, Milton walks in the back door. When he sees me, he raises his hands in the air and says, "I don't keep any money in the house."

I think he's kidding, but Milton is trembling.

Uh-oh. Danger ahead. I have been down this icy road before. It's one of the pitfalls of working with people in their eighties and nineties who want to write their memoirs before they die. Sometimes they forget who you are and what you're doing there. One time, a client called the cops on me—saying I was an intruder, and God what a lot of explaining I had to do.

No thank you. I don't want to spend the rest of my Sunday dealing with the police—or, worse, Milton's son. How am I going to justify my presence in the old man's house? Conrad will probably accuse me of breaking and entering—after all, wasn't I, a stranger, lurking outside his father's Brentwood home?

Why do things always get so complicated? Why do I have to deal with so many ancillary annoyances, when all I want to do is write?

"Milton, it's me, Dakota."

"How do you know my name?" he says in a whisper.

"I'm a ghostwriter. You hired me to write your life story."

The old man lets this sink in for a moment. I see a faint flicker in his eyes.

"Oh," he says, as if starting to remember. After a moment, he adds, "What are you doing here? It's Sunday."

"So you remember it's Sunday," I say, "but you don't recall asking me to come over."

"No, I don't."

"Do you remember me at all?"

"Faintly," he says, then plops into one of the teak kitchen

chairs. "Remind me what we talked about."

"I was here on Friday. You asked me to write a sixty-thousand-word book about your life. You gave me a folder of research materials. You paid me four thousand dollars."

The last statement is like smelling salts to the old man's dementia.

"Never forget a debt," he says. "If this ever happens again, just say 'four thousand bucks,' and I'll snap out of it. Okay?"

"Okay."

"You'd better get going, Dorota. I want to take a nap."

"My name is Dakota," I say. I need to make sure he remembers who I am—and that I'm not an intruder.

"What did I say?" Milton asks.

"You called me Dorota."

"Oh, yes, Dorota. Polish girlfriend I once had. Lovely woman."

"Just remember. I'm Dakota—Dakota Donovan."

"Okay, Dakota. Now, go home and get to work. You've got eight weeks from last Friday to give me a sixty-thousand-word manuscript. I already paid you four grand to do it. You've got the folder. You've got all the interviews you're going to get from me. So get to work."

"Four thousand bucks," I say.

"You only need to say it if I start to slip," he tells me.

"When do you want to get together again?"

"Eight weeks."

"You don't want to see a partial draft?"

"Today is the tenth of August. Eight weeks from now is the first of October. See you then."

As I pick up the Ralph's shopping bag that holds Milton's confidential file and photo album, I ask, "By the way, Milton, what happened to the filing cabinet in your office?"

Milton replies, "Nothing that I know of."

"It's gone."

"That dirty thief!" Milton says, jumping to his feet. "I had all kinds of valuable Hollywood memorabilia in that cabinet. My bum son has been stealing things bit by bit to sell on ebay.

Now he takes it all. What a greedy bastard!"

This isn't the first or even the tenth time I've seen a family member take off with an old person's treasures. Family infighting always presents a threat to my presence in the equation—because the kids may think the old man (or woman) is spending too much money on the memoir and try to get rid of me.

"That fascist!" Milton says, pounding a fist on the kitchen's Hans Olsen teak table—making me almost shriek in pain.

"Please, Milton. Be careful. That table is a museum piece."

"It's just like when they took valuables before sending people to the gas chamber. That's what my son wants to do to me—take everything, have me declared incompetent, grab my assets, and send me to a nursing home."

Milton starts to sob and covers his face with his hands. "I'm glad Geraldine isn't alive to see this. It would kill her."

I assume that Geraldine is Milton's deceased wife and Conrad's mother.

What can I say to comfort the poor old soul? What can I do?

"Milton, is there anybody I can call?" I hesitate about offering to help because I know I'll regret it. But I can't stop myself, and ask, "Is there anything I can do?"

"I want you to call my attorney," Milton says, wiping the tears on his cheeks with the swollen middle knuckle of each hand, "and tell him what happened. I'm going to sue that SOB if I have to."

"Milton, you don't want to sue your own son."

"He's Geraldine's son from before we were married."

"How old was Conrad when you married Geraldine?"

"Eighteen months."

"Then he's your son, Milton. You raised him."

"He's not like me. He's like his father, his real father."

I feel my hair roots—which need a touchup—start to tingle. A revelation—however minor—always gets my attention. I wait for Milton to go on, afraid if I say anything he might shut down.

Milton lets out a sigh that seems to fill the kitchen with tangible angst, and he shuffles out of the room as if to escape it.

34

gible angst, and he shuffles out of the room as if to escape it. He doesn't even turn around to see if I'm following him, making me wonder if he's forgotten that I'm here.

"Four thousand bucks," I call after him.

"I know you're here and who you are," he says without looking back.

I follow Milton to the living room, where I find him looking out the window holding a short glass of brown liquid in his hand. How many drinks has he had today? I don't want him to get bombed and fall after I leave.

"What's the occasion, Milton?" I say, thinking this might be a nonthreatening way to ask about the liquor.

But Milton doesn't bite. He has something else on his mind.

"Did you call my lawyer like I asked?"

"I don't know who your lawyer is," I say.

Milton turns and hands me a business card.

"Here," he says. "Call him."

"About what?"

"I remember what I told you, even if it happened a little while ago. My short-term memory stays with me sometimes. And this is one of those times."

"You want me to tell him that Conrad has been stealing from you."

"That's right."

"And what do you want the lawyer to do?"

"What else? Have the bum arrested."

"Maybe you can get the lawyer to work things out between you and your son."

"We're beyond that."

"Milton, I'm just a ghostwriter. I can't get involved in this."

"Then I want my four thousand back. And don't try to screw me. I know people."

"Milton, if I get involved, it will look bad."

"How so?"

"I just met you two days ago. If I insinuate myself into your personal life, your financial life, your conflict with your son, I'll look like a predatory gold-digger swooping down to take advantage of you."

"Since I got old, everybody takes advantage of me."

"I'm sorry, Milton. I really am."

"Even the cleaning ladies take things. One of them ran off with my Gerald Thurston lamp."

"So what happened?" I ask.

"About what?" Milton says, turning toward me—his cataracts looking opalescent in the light streaming through the window.

"When the cleaning lady tried to steal your lamp."

"How did you know about that?"

"Four thousand bucks," I say.

The clouds part in Milton's cataracts and a spark fires from somewhere deep down.

"Why do you want to know about this?" he asks.

"It's interesting," I tell him.

"Why are you so interested in what happens to other people?"

"It's what I do for a living, Milton. I write people's life stories."

"Sure you do it for a living. But you act like you really care about what people tell you."

"How else can I do a good job?"

"You'd better do a good job. I know people."

"And I know a few people myself," I say.

And for the first time all day, Milton's mouth arranges itself into a wicked smile. He even lets out half a laugh.

"I'm sure you do," he tells me, sinking into a Finn Juhl chair.

I want to ask Milton about so many things—his years in Army Intelligence, his midcentury modern collection, his deceased wife, his son, his business partner Duke Galveston, his career as a Hollywood producer, and, of course, the little men in the shiny silver suits. But once I start, I might be here for hours.

"Well," I say, "see you in October."

"It's only the tenth of August."

"You told me to . . ." then I realize that the old man has no recollection of what he'd said a short time before. I'll have to spend the next few months this way, never counting on anything he tells me.

"So when do you want to get together again? Not before two weeks, I hope that's okay with you."

But rather than respond, Milton's head drops to his chest and he lets out a resonating bass snore.

◀ SIX ▶

After sorting through Milton's confidential file the previous night, I'd reached my limit of even starting to absorb what was in it. I'd gone to bed with a sense of dread, the accordion folder my version of the albatross in the "Rime of the Ancient Mariner." But I wake up with a wonderful idea—to spend the day in the royal atmosphere of the Margaret Herrick Library in Beverly Hills, a research branch of the Academy of Motion Picture Arts and Sciences.

If so much of Milton's story involves Duke Galveston, why not visit the Margaret Herrick and dive into the facility's extensive material about this seminal figure in movie history—someone who'd arrived in the 1930s as an eighteen-year-old hayseed with money in his pocket and within a short time was producing and directing major motion pictures.

▼

I park in a metered spot behind the palatial red-roofed library—built in 1928 as the Beverly Hills waterworks and transformed into its current use in the 1970s—and feel myself becoming giddy at the thought of entering the facility. I love libraries, I love research—and this is the best library with the best staff in the most luxurious surroundings.

I need to get away from the daily grind and let my mind sink into my subject: Duke Galveston, the mystery man among mystery men.

As I'm feeding sixteen quarters into the meter—enough to buy four hours of parking—I hear someone yelling, but can't make out what the woman is saying. A shady, serene park area rests on the south end of the library grounds and many homeless people spend their days there under shady ficus trees.

The yelling gets louder, as if the person is getting closer. Some part of me knows who it is and what the person is saying, but the realization is slow in coming—as if I want to avoid the inevitable for as long as possible. Plunk, plunk, plunk go the quarters as I push them into the meter. Yell, scream, screech, goes the woman who's getting closer and closer and closer, until I can no longer avoid the collision with my shadow.

"DAKOTAAAAA! DAKOTAAAA! DAKOTAAA!"

With a slow turn of my head, I see Joyce, a homeless artist from my neighborhood, stumbling toward me in shocking pink patent leather stilettos, dressed in a lemon yellow sleeveless shift, and a pink, yellow, and orange flowered scarf. The middle-aged woman's long champagne-colored hair flies across her face as she lurches along.

She grabs a yellow pack of American Spirit cigarettes from the pocket of her dress, taps out a smoke, sticks it between her coral pink lips, reaches into her other pocket and pulls out an orange Bic lighter, fires it up, dips the cigarette to the flame, and treats herself to a greedy draw. I get the impression that Joyce has modeled her movements and attitude after Lauren Bacall's performances in 1940s films such as *To Have and Have Not* and *The Big Sleep*.

"How come I haven't seen you around the neighborhood?" she asks.

"I've been busy, Joyce," I say walking toward the library entrance.

"You promised to let me draw your portrait," she says, referring to her main source of income—street portraits and cartoons.

Joyce gets in step beside me and puffs away, strutting and puffing as if she's strolling up the red carpet of the world. Even after a year as a nonsmoker, I'm tempted each day to run out for cigarettes. A major boon about not smoking is that your hair and clothes no longer smell like smoke. But I'm sure as hell going to reek inside the library now that Joyce has unleashed her smoke bomb. I wave my hands in front of myself, trying to move the smoke from the still air—never a breeze in L.A.—hoping that Joyce will get the message and either put out the cigarette or stop following me.

It's about a two-block walk to the entrance, so Joyce has plenty of time to strut and puff—and I have more than enough time to soak up the stink.

"They won't let me in this place," Joyce says, nodding toward the library, "because I don't have a driver's license. And I need something from in there."

I close my eyes, lean my head back, and sigh.

"I want you to get a picture from the Marilyn Monroe file," Joyce says. "I need a copy of that photo where the breeze is blowing up her white dress. People tell me I can make a lot of money if I start selling drawings like that on the Walk of Fame."

▼

I've been to the Margaret Herrick Library a few times and am familiar with the institution's requirements and procedures. But on my first visit, the protocol came as a shock.

In effect, you leave your life at the door. After showing your driver's license or passport and signing in, the clerk gives you a key and directs you to a small room filled with lockers for your belongings. If you're a woman, that means your purse, jacket, computer case, pens, pencils. The library allows you to retain two items: your laptop and I.D.

You climb a staircase to a second floor where the library is located. There, you sign in again with an official librarian. In exchange for your driver's license, you receive a daily pass. The idea is that if you try to run off with anything, you'll have to take the bus home, where the cops will be waiting for you.

The librarian checks your laptop to make sure nothing is hidden in it. Then you receive a short pencil and scraps of paper about the size of a cigarette pack—yes, I now have cigarettes on the brain. The library allows you to use your laptop to take notes—for the institution, it's safer than pencils, which could slip and deface its precious materials.

I decide to get Joyce off of my mind by taking care of her request before starting to research Duke Galveston. I sit at one of the computer terminals and look up the Marilyn Monroe flick *The Seven Year Itch*, learn it came out in 1955—then go up to the research desk and fill out a request for the file.

While I wait, I use my computer to visit imdb.com, and look up the titles of movies that Duke Galveston produced or directed. I fill out a form to request the materials—always, as I'd learned on previous visits, in alphabetical order. Next, I make out a form for Duke Galveston's biographical materials. I decide to start with these, and if I have time review the movie files.

"Dakota," a man's voice calls.

I get up and approach the research desk and the librarian—a man in his late thirties with movie star looks perfect for the surroundings—hands me *The Seven Year Itch* file, which I bring to a table and flip through, taking less than a minute to locate the "Marilyn above the ventilation grate" photo by Sam Shaw. Hallelujah! After filling out a request for a photocopy, I return the folder and put in my order for the Duke Galveston biographical files.

The librarian shakes his head when he sees the request.

"We have hundreds of files on Galveston, most of it on microfilm."

I have to resist the urge to groan. How I hate dealing with the microfiche monster. That fricking leviathan always jams, and I spend hours wrestling with it and get nothing done. Damn. But I can't seem rude, can I?

"I'm looking forward to reviewing the material," I say.

"Do you have any specific dates in mind?" the librarian asks. I look at his nameplate—Derrick Richards—even his name sounds marquee-ready.

I think about Derrick's question for a few moments. Milton started working with Duke Galveston after WWII. Might as well begin in 1942 and find out what Galveston was doing during the war.

After I give Derrick my answer, he smiles and nods.

"Dakota!" I hear a man's voice call.

I make my way to another desk, where a pudgy man with a blond crew cut holds out a sheet of paper—the photocopy of the Marilyn Monroe photo by Sam Shaw. The man asks for my name, address, and phone number, then makes out an invoice for the twenty-five cent purchase.

I hold out a quarter, but before taking it, the researcher asks: "What do you intend to do with this photo?"

"Intend?"

"What are your plans for the photo?"

"I'm a researcher," I say, giving one of my standard non-committal answers.

"That's not what I asked."

"Well . . ." I look at the man's shirt pocket to see if he's wearing a name badge. But, of course, this isn't a Jiffy Lube—it's the Margaret Herrick Library.

" . . . Wilson," he says.

"Well, Wilson, I'm not sure about my plans for the photo. Why do you ask?"

"If you intend to draw or paint a reproduction of this image, you will be guilty of copyright infringement."

"I don't draw."

"If this copy is used by anyone to infringe on the photographer's copyright, you will be held responsible."

WTF, I think. Now I've got to worry about the freaking copyright police? I'm temped to say: *Perhaps you haven't heard, holed away in this exclusive enclave, that there's this thing, the Internet, where you can find any effing picture you want and print it out in the privacy of your home and draw with infringing glee.* I can't say that. I'll need Wilson's help throughout the day, and besides I don't want to risk getting kicked out of the place or banned for life. Yes, there is such a fate for attempted theft—the place prides itself on no one ever getting away with anything.

I think of a semi-truth—different from a semi-lie. My daughter took a sewing class where they'd made a copy of the white halter dress Marilyn had worn in the photo. I can say the class is happening now and my daughter needs a copy of the photo. But, again, wouldn't Flannery have received a copy in her sewing class or obtained one from the Internet? I decide to tell the truth.

"A homeless woman in my neighborhood asked me to get her a copy of the photo. I ran into her outside. She doesn't have access to the Internet and can't get in here because she doesn't have a driver's license."

"And why does she want the photo?"

"She loves Marilyn Monroe. She's a big fan. I think she plans to keep the photo as a good luck charm."

Wilson's pupils widen as if his eyes are camera lenses trying to get me in focus. I know he's deciding whether he buys my story. God, all this time wasted, I think, and I haven't even started the Duke Galveston research. I feel a migraine coming on and realize that my purse is in the locker downstairs—but, anyway, I didn't fortify myself with medication.

Before Wilson can mete out his judgment, I ask, "Do you have any Excedrin?"

"We are not allowed to dispense medication of any kind."

I take a deep breath, then let out a loud yawn—sending everyone in the place looking in my direction. Yes, I have a big, big, big migraine coming on—and big yawns, my brain's way of trying to get more oxygen, are my advance warning. What should I do, what in the hell should I do? Should I try to get through a couple of the Duke Galveston biographical files, or should I leave now and try to get home before the thunderbolts hit? God forbid that I have to pull over and lie in the back seat until the worst of the headache passes, which could take hours.

Oh, damn, the Escher staircases, I'm seeing the Escher staircases in front of me—yes, this is going to be a very bad migraine. And I just had one two days ago! Double damn!

If only I could find somebody carrying Excedrin. But nobody is carrying anything.

I don't want to leave! I want to have fun going through the Duke Galveston files!

"Excuse me," I hear a woman say, "I have some."

I turn and see a tall, elegant blonde woman who looks like Grace Kelly if the actress had lived twenty years longer.

"Excedrin?" I ask.

The woman nods and says, "Come with me."

We make our way down the stairs to the little room with the lockers. While my companion retrieves the pain relievers, I open my locker and pull out a stainless steel thermos of cold water.

After the woman hands over the green Excedrin bottle, I tap out two tablets and swallow them with a gulp of water. I take a couple of deep breaths, then sigh.

I turn and look at the merciful stranger.

"I think I may have caught it in time," I say.

"We can only hope," the woman says and smiles. She has the throaty voice of a Kathleen Turner. I've always wanted a voice like that. I've tried to tone down my Midwestern accent since moving to L.A., but still speak with the broad vowels and clipped consonants that mark me as a California outsider.

The woman holds out her hand and says, "I'm Shelby Norris." Then she adds, "I couldn't help overhearing you asking about the Duke Galveston files . . ."

◄ SEVEN ►

When Shelby Norris mentions that I'm researching Duke Galveston, I feel sick. I should have been more discreet when requesting the files. Now it's out that somebody is writing about the deceased tycoon. This is not good, not good at all. What if the people who scared Milton into silence for over thirty years find out about this? Wait, I tell myself, calm down, don't worry. Take a breath.

I figure the elderly blonde must be a famous something or somebody, but don't want to embarrass myself by asking what. I decide to make a guess.

"The screenwriter?" making a wild guess based on the sound of her name.

"My dear," the woman says, "there is only one Shelby Norris."

"Pleased to meet you," I say, then introduce myself and thank the woman for the Excedrin.

Shelby puts the Excedrin in her purse, takes out a merlot-colored lipstick and touches up her lips. After fluffing up her blonde curls, she leans against the lockers, crosses her arms, and tilts her head as if posing for a newspaper photo: *Legendary Hollywood screenwriter visits old stomping grounds.* She taps the heel of her beige pump against the granite floor and says, "If you don't mind my asking, what's your business with Galveston?"

"Research," I say.

"Come on," Shelby says, raising one eyebrow, "you can do better than that."

"I'm working on a project," I answer. "That's all I can say."

Shelby pushes herself away from the lockers, puts her hands on her hips, and faces me, staring into my eyes.

I'm already bleary-eyed from an incipient migraine and don't need an angry stare aimed into my sockets. Shelby is looking straight into my eyes, so I figure she must be a tiny woman—since she's in three-inch heels and I'm wearing flat-heeled boots.

"Is somebody writing another biography of Duke Galveston?" Shelby asks. When I don't respond, she adds, "Hasn't enough ink been wasted maligning that poor soul?"

"So you knew Duke Galveston?"

"I should."

"And why is that?"

"For Christ's sake, I was married to the man."

I know the outlines of Duke Galveston's biography. He was married twice—once to a hometown Texas girl when he was eighteen, and twice to actress Joan Paulson. I've never read about a marriage to Shelby Norris. But I don't mention that. I have something more important to ask.

"Would you be willing to give me an interview?"

Twenty minutes later, I'm sitting across from Shelby Norris at a table in the corner of a crowded—and pricy—Beverly Hills bistro. I'd tried to set up a meeting for another time, at another place—say, a coffee shop, where I wouldn't go broke doing the interview. But Shelby had offered to treat me to lunch at one of her favorite 90210 spots.

My migraine has escalated to the next level, despite the Excedrin. I'm now experiencing extreme sensitivity to light, sounds, and smells—and the last place I want to visit is a bright, loud, garlic-reeking restaurant. But I can't pass up the chance to interview Duke Galveston's former wife, can I?

"I used to come here with Duke," Shelby says. "He loved this place."

Whoa, I think. Duke Galveston out in public? Eating at a restaurant? Doesn't Shelby know that Duke was recluse who subsisted on a diet of equal-sized peas and quarter-inch bites of steak?

"He did." I say the two words as a statement, voiced with skepticism. Shelby picks up on my tone.

"You don't believe all that tripe you've heard about poor, dear Duke, do you?"

"You tell me," I say.

I rest my elbow on the table and push on my left temple to put pressure on the headache. The table wobbles as I press on my forehead, sending my glass of ice water sliding off the edge. I reach out with my right hand and catch the glass mid-fall.

"Quick reflexes," Shelby notes.

"I'm thirsty," I tell her, and gulp down most of the water. Then I hold the glass of ice to the left side of my head and let out a big yawn. God, what a horrible lunch companion I am.

"Maybe this was a bad idea," Shelby says, patting her puffy blonde tresses.

"I'm so sorry," I tell her and mean it. I'm sorry I have a migraine and sorry I'm ruining any chance at an interview.

"Maybe we should leave," Shelby suggests.

"I can't leave now. I can't drive."

"Well, then, do you mind if I eat?"

▼

After three cups of espresso and two carafes of ice water, my migraine is easing up. I've even managed to down a few forkfuls of linguini topped with olive oil and Parmesan—at twenty-five dollars, something I didn't want to order, but Shelby had insisted, reiterating that it was her "treat." All the various headache remedies—Excedrin, coffee, ice, and even a few bites of carbs—have helped.

While waiting for our food, Shelby spends ten minutes sticking books of matches under the table base, trying to fix the wobble—making me wonder if she, like Duke Galveston, suffers from Obsessive Compulsive Disorder. When the food arrives, Shelby digs into her slab of lasagna and side of antipasto as if she was just released from the hull of a slave ship.

Looking at the woman's svelte figure, I would have assumed that she consumes about one hundred calories per day—maybe an unsalted rice cake, a couple of romaine leaves, and a teaspoon of yogurt. But, instead, Shelby has probably ingested over a thousand calories in just one meal. She devours everything down to the last morsel of minced garlic, which she soaks up with Italian bread.

It's always difficult to conduct an interview over a meal because most people prefer not to eat and talk at the same time. I usually direct the interview subject to eat while I offer some background on the project or throw out questions we can discuss over coffee.

"Shelby," I begin, "I really appreciate your offering to answer some questions about . . ."

Before I can say "Duke Galveston," Shelby raises her finger to her lips and looks around to see if anybody is listening to our conversation.

I lower my voice to a whisper and say, "Your former husband."

"Go ahead. Ask away," Shelby says, as she checks her lipstick and teeth in a silver compact, then looks around for the waiter, who's busy at another table.

"First off," I say, "did Duke ever mention working with a Milton Kingman?"

"Duke worked with thousands of people over the years—in the oil business, in the entertainment business, and in the electronics and defense businesses."

"I understand that," I say. "But I'm talking about an individual who played a special role in Duke's life. He was what you might call a silent partner in some top-secret businesses."

"What's the name again?"

"Milton Kingman."

"Milton. Milton," Shelby repeats, raising her eyes to the ceiling as if the answer is written there. Then she turns her gaze toward me and says, "Is he a rather small man? Someone who would now be close to ninety?"

I nod.

"Yes," Shelby says, "I met him. He used to come to the house in Bel Air."

"When was this?"

"During the fifties."

"How often did they meet?"

"I have no idea."

"How many times that you know about?"

"Maybe half a dozen."

I'm feeling much, much better. Nothing lifts my mood like a hard-to-get interview that confirms an important fact—in this case, that Duke Galveston worked with Milton. The old man isn't delusional, at least not about this.

"What do you think they were working on?" I whisper, leaning toward Shelby.

"Something hush-hush," Shelby says. "At first, I thought it had to do with Duke's other women, using someone to pass along messages. But I realized there had to be more to it."

"What made you think that?" I say.

I'm fighting the urge to take notes. Sometimes, especially when someone is telling me something I really want to know, the person stops talking when I begin to take notes. The interview subject snaps out of the spell and realizes he or she has said more than intended.

Shelby holds up her arm and waves, finally catching the waiter's attention. I want an answer before the waiter arrives, and repeat my question: "What made you think there was something hush-hush going on?"

"They'd work in Duke's study and Milton always brought a steamer trunk with him. He rolled it in on a dolly, and the trunk was all locked up with straps and padlocks."

"Didn't you ask what was in the trunk?" I prod, looking over my shoulder and seeing that the waiter is just steps away.

"Of course," Shelby tells me.

"And . . ."

"And . . . Duke said that Milton was bringing over scale models for him to review."

"Scale models of what?"

"I don't know."

"Did you have any ideas, any hunches? Did you overhear any conversations?"

"Push, push, push," Shelby says, glaring at Dakota. "You writers are all alike."

"I thought you were a writer," I say.

"That's how I know."

Before I can respond, the actor-working-as-a-waiter-while-waiting-for-a-break arrives at the table.

"Dessert?" the beauteous waiter asks, as he gestures for the busboy to clear the plates.

I start to decline, but Shelby has room for more—"dessert?" is not a question, but a foregone conclusion.

"Tiramisu, cappuccino gelato, two forks, two spoons."

The waiter nods, smiles, and leaves to fetch the treats for the middle-aged woman with the migraine, and the elderly woman with the bottomless stomach.

"Are you like one of those pythons that eats one big meal every couple of weeks?"

"Three meals a day for me," Shelby says.

"But how do you . . ." I begin, then stop myself from asking how Shelby stays so slim, thinking maybe the remark is too personal. Anyway, I need to stay on the subject: Shelby's former husband, Duke Galveston.

"Can you tell me when you and Duke were married?" I ask.

"Between his first and second marriages to Joan Paulson," Shelby answers. "You can look up the dates on imdb. I'm at an age when I need to verify all my memories via google, imdb, or wikipedia."

"With all due respect, Shelby, I have looked up Duke on imdb and didn't see you listed as a wife."

"We were married at sea. After we split up, Duke's people paid off the ship's captain to destroy the evidence."

"Were you bitter about the breakup?"

"I knew it couldn't last. I was one of the few blondes Duke ever dated, let alone lived with. He loved brunettes, and Joan Paulson was his ideal type. When she decided to come back to him, I never stood a chance."

"How did he break off the relationship?"

"He gave me the house in Bel Air, but that's long gone. It's funny that Duke made sure all of his mistresses had homes, but more than a few ended up broke and homeless . . ."

After Shelby's voice trails off, she sits back in her chair.

"Excuse me for a moment," Shelby says, patting her lips with her napkin, picking up her doggie bag—an extra meal she'd ordered for later—and strutting off toward the ladies room.

"Oh," I think. That's another possibility for why a big eater like Shelby is so slim. But would a bulimic have lived this long? Then again, I can't assume the woman is going into the restroom to say hello and goodbye to the meal she's just eaten. But that's what I do for a living—make judgments based on clues and evidence. In essence, I'm a private detective ferreting out the facts and truths of people's lives.

While Shelby is in the restroom, I take notes about what I've just heard. The waiter brings the tiramisu and gelato, but I let the dessert sit there, waiting for Shelby to return. As I make notes, I slip into a writer's trance, jotting down ideas that Shelby's comments have sparked. (Did Shelby write scripts for any of Duke Galveston's films? How did the two met? Did she know any of Duke Galveston's other women? Does she know anyone else I can interview about Duke?)

When I look up, the gelato has melted, no one is sitting across from me, and the waiter is presenting a black folder that contains the check. I place the folder on the other side of the table, but the waiter again sets it in front of me.

"My friend is buying lunch," I say, looking up at a man I'm sure has auditioned to play an action figure or superhero.

"I'm afraid your friend left about fifteen minutes ago."

"Left?"

The waiter pushes the black folder toward me. I open it: $101.80—without the tip. There is no way I can pay this. My credit card is maxed out and I only have eight dollars and some change on me. I don't carry checks.

"I'm sorry," I say. "I can't pay for this right now. I'll have to come back."

The waiter—perhaps practicing for a role as a law enforcement professional—narrows his gaze, crosses his arms over his chest, and says, "You're going to have to pay."

After he threatens to call the Beverly Hills Police, who he says, "Look down on this sort of thing," I remember that I can pay with my debit card.

Well, there goes paying the phone bill.

◀ EIGHT ▶

My migraine is gone, but now I'm wired on all the espresso I've swilled to get rid of it. I don't feel like sitting in my car for an hour while driving home in the heat with no a/c—it's not worth paying fifteen hundred dollars to have it fixed—so I decide to go back to the Margaret Herrick Library, which is open for another three hours.

After checking in and depositing my belongings in a locker, I again ascend the stairway to heaven—at least my idea of paradise. As I hand over my driver's license to the receptionist, who reminds me of a younger version of Egyptian actor Omar Sharif, I ask if he's seen Shelby Norris and offer a brief description of the woman.

"She was here before," the receptionist says. "I saw the two of you talking about Excedrin."

I figure everybody who works in the library has to be hyper alert, searching, searching, searching for potential thieves. I assume this man observes a lot while he's at the desk.

"Right," I say, trying to force a smile, "she gave me Excedrin for my migraine. But I need to talk to her about something else."

The receptionist, whose nametag reads "Jerrold," shrugs.

"How often does she come here?" I ask.

"I really can't divulge any information about our visitors."

I sigh and trudge back to the reference desk. It won't do any good to use a direct approach. I'll have to slide the question into a casual conversation with one of the librarians or a patron.

After requesting the Duke Galveston files from Derrick, who looks even more handsome in the afternoon light, I find a table and wait for someone to call my name.

About five minutes later, Wilson—the buzz-cut researcher from earlier in the day—shouts out "Day Kota" (in contrast to "Night Kota") and when I gather the files try to bait him with a few questions about Shelby Norris, but he doesn't bite.

When I flip open the folder, I see that it's filled with microfilm strips and have to fight the urge to groan—the opposite of my migraine yawn where I'm trying to take in oxygen. My groans can be epic expressions of utter disgust, my body trying to clear itself of bad vibes. No, I tell myself. You've already released a sonic-boom yawn in this quiet enclave, if you pull another ditty out of your sound repertoire, the powers that be may bar you for life. Still, I can't help but let out a little one, which sounds like "eeehhhyaaa."

Now, to face the dreaded microfiche.

▼

After two hours struggling with microfilm, I've printed out about thirty pages of articles and photos featuring Duke Galveston. I want to print many more pages, but only have eight dollars with me, and the copies cost twenty-five cents each. I'm nearing my budget limit and the library is still open for another hour.

While I take a Duke Galveston tour via microfilm, I fall into my concentration fugue, where I don't know what time it is or how much time has passed. The concentration fugue is similar to my writer's coma in that I have no sense of my surroundings or what's going on around me.

But like a buzzing fly, something keeps humming around me, something is drawing me out, out, out of what I'm doing. I try to swat away the intrusion with an old trick—blinking my eyes as a form of self-hypnosis to take me back under the spell, but after a couple of tries I'm, boom, back in the present in a stuffy closet-sized space—only now I realize I'm not alone. A man in his mid-forties is sitting at the microfilm reader to the left of me, only he isn't looking at his screen—he's craning his neck to see what I'm reading.

I spot all this with my peripheral vision. I keep moving through the microfilm for a while so the man doesn't know that while he's watching me, I'm watching him. Good God, I think, he's even taking notes. Or am I getting paranoid? When Milton hired me for this ghostwriting gig, he gave me enough fodder for that, so it's not all in my mind. I tell myself that maybe the guy is just glancing around while taking notes on his own material.

More than once I've received glares, glowers, and scowls from people who thought I was staring at them, when I was just staring into space while gathering my thoughts. I can't decide whether or not the man is watching me, or if he's just lost in space, so I figure there's only one thing to do.

I turn and look him full in the face. The man exhibits a slight blip, a fleeting movement to show that I've caught him off-guard and that he has, in fact, been watching me. Over the years, I've spent thousands of hours interviewing people and have built up a library of expressions, body language, movements, blips, tics, and other behavior—and have drawn conclusions about what these traits indicate. To get at the truth about people, I've had to become a behavioralist and cultural anthropologist, in addition to my roles as confessor, confidante, devil's advocate, psychologist, sister, mother, aunt, daughter—the writing is the least of it.

After the man's minor hesitation reveals his intentions, he looks away, back at his own microfilm screen—giving me a chance to observe him.

He has an arty air—and I feel certain he is a writer in some way, shape, or form: screenwriter, biographer, playwright, journalist. He has longish dark hair and wears a vintage gray suit from the 1960s—along with short black boots. I figure him for at least six feet tall, judging by the length of his legs. I note all this in a few blinks of my eyes—in addition to my other roles as ghostwriter, I've also had to develop the observation skills of a journalist.

As I turn back to my microfilm screen, I hear the man say in a low, soothing voice, "How's your headache?"

That's the last thing I expected him to say, if he said anything at all.

"Does everyone in this place know I had a headache?" I say turning to him. I'm trying not to smile, but can't manage it.

"Well, you were speaking in a very loud voice when you were asking for Excedrin."

"Oh, right," I say, "this is a library. I should have whispered. Then again, I had a very loud headache."

"So I take it you're feeling better," the man says, looking into my eyes. The room is dark and for a moment I picture the exchange accompanied by glasses of pinot noir.

"After mucho espresso and Excedrin, my headache is gone, but I'll be up for days."

The man smiles, as if he finds me the cleverest person he's ever met. He stands up, reaches out his hand, and says, "I'm Riley Taylor."

I put my hand in his and shake. His hand is warm and a spark flies between us. We both feel the charge and smile at the same time.

"And you are . . ." he says.

"If you heard me screaming for headache remedies, you must have heard Wilson yelling my name."

"Your name is Daytona?"

"Yes, and you can guess my last name."

"Louisiana?"

"You need a geography lesson," I say.

"Daytona Florida? That's your name?"

"According to Wilson."

As if waiting for his cue, Wilson rushes into room, and fills up the tiny, dim space with an extended, "Shhhh," then adds, "people are trying to concentrate!"

Before we have a chance to respond, Wilson turns on his heel like a pudgy soldier doll and propels himself out of the room.

I make an exaggerated grimace and put a finger to my lips. I point to my microfilm screen and whisper, "Back to work."

As I click through more filmstrips, depicting Duke Galveston in his midyears, a sheet of white paper soars into my lap, as if it has flown there. When I look down, I see in block letters: 7000 ICEBERG—and when I look up, my companion is gone.

I step to the doorway and stare into the large, open space where researchers are bent over folders, files, and stacks of papers, sifting, sifting, sifting for facts, figures, secrets, tidbits, juicy morsels. But Riley isn't there, so I walk into the main area and look down the length of the space, all the way to the end where they keep the interview transcripts. The man is gone, almost as if he's never been here.

And what is 7000 Iceberg?

As I head back to the microfilm viewing room, I wonder what it means. I figure the phrase must have something to do with my research subject: billionaire tycoon/movie mogul Duke Galveston. I rush back to my microfilm machine and pick up the pile of articles and photos I've printed out. After a few shuffles through the deck, there it is: An article about the 1974 break-in at Duke Galveston's headquarters at 7000 Iceberg Street in West Hollywood.

◄ NINE ►

Thirty minutes later, I'm crawling along in the West Hollywood afternoon rush. Through the windshield, I stare at the bleached-out sky, imagining it as a blank sheet of paper, where, voila!, words will appear to explain it all—everything that has ever puzzled or perplexed me.

I play many mental games as I drive, to keep my mind off the heat, my lack of air conditioning, and the general sensation I have of boiling like a lobster in my car.

I'm so caught up in imagining the smoggy sky as paper and the palm trees as gigantic pens that I almost miss my turn: Iceberg Street. I make a left onto the narrow two-lane drag and try to keep from colliding with the SUVs, Hummers, and pickup trucks bulging over the center line.

With my challenged sense of depth perception—really, almost a complete lack thereof—it's a mammoth challenge for me to read the addresses on the buildings while driving, avoiding collisions, and keeping track of whose turn it is to move ahead at four-way stops. But from a block away I spot 7000 Iceberg Street—Duke Galveston's headquarters back in the day, his art deco, small-scale White House.

As I approach the building, a car pulls out from a spot near the entrance and I slip into the space. It's six o'clock and the day is still set on "hot, no steam," but I figure as long as I'm here it's a good idea to look around—one more thing to cross off my research list. But when I try to open my driver's side door, it won't budge. The veins in my throat start to throb—and I wonder if this is the kind of panic people feel when trapped in a submarine. I have a horrible thought: What if this car is so old, with hinges so rusty, that the doors won't open anymore?

I scoot over the center console and the emergency brake and scuttle to the passenger door, saying a complete "Hail Mary" before pulling on the handle. Ah, the beautiful sound of the door creaking open.

I feel strange exiting the car on the passenger side, as if I'm entering another dimension. When I get out and shut the Toyota's door, I say another complete "Hail Mary" that it will open again.

As I walk toward the entrance of 7000 Iceberg, I look up at the edifice—smooth white surface with tan accents, a quintessential California color combination, cool, calm, and oh-so collected. I wonder who or what now occupies the building.

A voice inside my head says, "Go home—now!" But I try to reason with myself: "As long as I'm here, I may as well look around."

Even though Duke Galveston never worked out of this building—his command center was a bungalow at the Beverly Hilton or a hotel room in Las Vegas—7000 Iceberg Street is still entwined with his persona as a man of mystery. I should make an attempt to at least get through the door.

So with a dry mouth and a parched throat, I march up the front walk, turn left, and make my way toward the entrance of 7000 Iceberg Street. But as I'm about to push on the door handle, I feel a hand on my left shoulder and let out a yell that registers at least an octave above high C.

When I spin around, I see Riley Taylor, the man from the microfilm room at the Margaret Herrick Library.

"I think I just saved you from getting arrested for breaking and entering," he says, with a smile that reveals a row of glaring teeth—the work, I'm sure, of a bleach-happy Beverly Hills dentist.

"You're the one who gave me the address," I respond, trying to spot his eyes behind his sunglasses—but the lenses are dark green, impossible to see through.

Riley puts his hand under my left elbow and guides me down the pathway toward the sidewalk.

"I was afraid you might think I was telling you to storm the castle," he whispers. "So I decided to come over and check. And there you were."

"There I were," I say, eliciting a laugh from my companion.

"Come on," Riley says, looking up and down the block, "we'd better get out of here."

"You make this sound like a spy caper," I say.

"Something like that," he tells me.

▼

Twenty minutes later, I'm sitting across from Riley at the Revolution Wine Bar on Melrose, a few blocks from the Iceberg Street location. We'd walked rather than try to find a parking spot in the busy West Hollywood nightlife district.

It's still early, before the dinner rush, and we sit in the half-occupied bistro over glasses of chilled Pinot Blanc and a twenty-five-dollar cheese plate—Reblochon, Idiázabel, Manchego, Mahon, and Blue D'auvergne.

I have no idea about the man's motives or reason for asking to talk to me. But I don't want to pose a direct question—I've learned over the years that a direct question is a way of revealing too much. I'll wait until he says something—other than making comments about the weather (hot), the wine (chilled), the cheese (room temperature), and the restaurant (cool). Ah, well, as long as I don't get stuck with the bill, the man can remain as laconic as he wishes. And he can keep his sunglasses on forever, for that matter.

While I reach for a wedge of Manchego, Riley slides off his sunglasses, sets them on the table, puts his finger on my chin—tilting up my face so I'm looking in his eyes—and says, "So what are your plans for this evening?"

"I want to walk back to my car before the sun sets," I reply—not as a flip answer, but because I'm concerned about visiting the deserted side street after dark.

Riley reaches into his inside jacket pocket and pulls out a silver pocket-watch emblazoned with fleurs-de-lis. He opens the cover to reveal a silver face with black Roman numerals.

"It's still early," he says, snapping shut the watch and sliding it back into his pocket.

"Is that your Boy Scout watch?" I ask.

Riley crinkles his eyes and tilts his head to one side, as if puzzled. "What makes you say that?"

"The fleur de lis. Isn't that the Boy Scouts emblem?"

"Is it?"

"So saving me from breaking and entering at 7000 Iceberg was your good deed for the day."

"The night is young. I may have a few more good deeds in me."

I try to figure out if this is intended as a clever remark or a lewd comment. That's the thing about writers—we can parse each word or phrase for hours. Still, this one isn't that ambiguous. But I choose to ignore it and give him the benefit of the doubt, with two strikes called at the plate. I decide to draw him out while giving away as little as possible about myself.

"And my good deeds start right here, right now," Riley says.

"Yes, the cheese plate is sublime," I tell him.

I love cheese but rarely eat any because—along with red wine and garlic—it's one of my migraine triggers.

He leans across the table and whispers, "You know what I mean."

I fight the urge to laugh or smile at Riley's conspiratorial manner and tone. My cheeks hurt from trying to hold them in place. I clamp my lips together so a laugh doesn't escape or a smile doesn't erupt. I blink a few times to keep my face from giving away my thoughts, then shake my head and say, "No idea."

Riley pushes back his chair and puts his hands on the sides of the table as if planning to pin me in with it. He lets his hands rest there for a moment before starting to drum on the tabletop with his fingertips.

"I think you have a few ideas," he tells me.

I shake my head and say, "Why don't you tell me what you're talking about, and I'll see if anything comes to mind."

Riley picks up his wine and starts to take a sip, but sets it down and instead lifts his glass of ice water and takes a few gulps. He looks to his right and to his left, then leans in close and speaks in a near whisper.

"I know who you're working for," he says, staring into my eyes.

His eyes are a murky green—impossible to fathom. My

eyes are light blue and easy to read. I glance away, then pick up his sunglasses from the table and put them on. I'm not about to have this conversation without some kind of cover.

"And your point is . . ." I begin.

"My point is that you'd be wise to return Milton Kingman's money and run from this gig as fast as you can."

I respond with a bland, "Is that so?" I'm not going to register shock, surprise, or even interest—and will continue to offer vague, noncommittal responses.

"You don't know what you've stumbled across, Dakota," Riley says, touching the back of my hand for a brief moment, as if trying to gain my confidence and make me believe in his good intentions.

"You've lost me," I say.

He leans closer, so that his upper body extends all the way across the table. "You know exactly what I'm talking about," he says.

I look toward the window, then pull off Riley's Ray-Bans, set them on the table, and say, "Well, it'll be dark soon. I'd better get going."

When I stand up, he grabs my left forearm and holds it.

"We need to talk," he says. Then he lets go of my arm, stares up at me, and adds, "We *really* need to talk."

"I'm not talking."

"Then just sit down for five more minutes and listen."

I tell myself not to give into curiosity, but can't resist. Anyway, it's just for five minutes. I sit down.

I wait, but Riley doesn't saying anything. Then he inhales for a long, long breath as if preparing for a deep-sea dive without an oxygen tank.

"Okay," he says, "this is the short version. A few months ago, Milton Kingman interviewed me about ghostwriting his memoirs. He let me review a large folder of documents, along with hundreds of photographs. But before we got started, Kingman said he'd changed his mind, that he wanted to, as he put it, 'let sleeping dogs lie.' But the story, what I'd learned of it anyway, had sort of taken me over and I said to myself, 'Why not write about this on your own?' The deeper I dug, the more obvious it became that there were people out there, powerful people who didn't want this story told."

"And what's the story?" I ask.

"You've talked to Kingman. You've seen his file and his photos. You've done research on Duke Galveston You must have some ideas."

"I'm not going to comment on what you think you know or what you think I know," I say. "But since you think you know who I am and what I do, I'll mention that I take my work seriously. There's attorney/client privilege, the sanctity of the confessional, the right of a journalist to protect sources, and there's ghostwriter confidentiality. That's all I have to say."

I stand up and Riley follows. He motions to the waiter for the check as he shadows me to the exit.

At the doorway, I say, "Thanks for the wine and cheese."

"Wait for me to pay the bill," he says. "I'll walk you to your car."

"It's not dark yet."

"I need to say a few more things. Please. It's important."

Again, my curiosity starts to churn. Pandora that I am, my desire to unlock secrets and learn the truth has driven me into more crazy, difficult, outrageous situations than I can count—what's one more?

While Riley Taylor pays the check with his American Express gold card—and what self-respecting book writer is solvent enough to merit one of those?—I stroll back to the table and pick up his pair of two hundred dollar Ray-Bans, which he no doubt can afford to lose. But who am I to criticize? I spent almost as much for lunch with Shelby Norris, someone I now figure for a total fraud who's never seen more than a photo of Duke Galveston.

I look at the twenty-five-dollar plate of cheese—with nary a nibble out of it. What a waste. But I'm not about to ask for a doggie—or mousie—bag. Anyway, it isn't my fault the cheese is going to waste when poor starving children in Wisconsin would love to have it. Right now, someone who can afford to waste money is paying for the pricey fromage.

When I look up, Riley is standing in the doorway in the last threads of sunlight. I hold up his sunglasses to show that I've remembered what he's forgotten, then make my way to the door.

I watch as Riley glances out the window. He takes a step back, turns and looks at me, mouths "sorry," and bolts out the door. By the time I reach the sidewalk, he's gone. I'm still holding his sunglasses, which I stuff into the front pocket of my purse.

I look up and down the block, then across the street, where I see a man in a black hoodie and sunglasses standing by the curb. It's too hot for a hoodie and too late for sunglasses.

Holy Mary Mother of God, pray for us sinners, I recite as I turn and make my way to 7000 Iceberg Street in the steely twilight.

Well, I think, as I rush toward my destination, Riley ran off, but at least he didn't run out on the check. Twice in one day would have eaten up a month's grocery budget.

I want to turn around to see if black hoodie is following me, but feel certain he is. The back of my neck is stiff and prickly, as if it has sent out antennae to detect any hint of danger—which now registers high on the scale.

To keep calm, I try self-talk—a technique I'd learned while ghostwriting a book about Behavioral Emotive Therapy—telling myself that there are plenty of people on the street and that would deter most criminals, wouldn't it?

◀ TEN ▶

A Tangent Store looms ahead, and as I head toward the mass merchandiser I weigh several options. Should I dip into Tangent and try to lose my pursuer—or just sprint to my car in the dark? I decide to turn around and see who's behind me before making up my mind.

I turn. I look. I make up my mind.

As I run into the store, I'm moving so fast that I kick myself in the shin. It feels fitting—I deserve it for even leaving my apartment this morning.

From the corner of my eye, I see stainless steel pots and pans shining from a pegboard. I figure the kitchenware department also features an assortment of sharp knives. If I can find one for less than ten dollars—all the credit that remains on my credit card—I'll buy it.

This is the first time in my life I've considered buying a weapon of any kind. Maybe I should try a baseball bat—less chance of stabbing myself. But where's the sporting goods department? The fricking store is so vast that I could wander for hours looking for a Louisville Slugger—which probably costs way more than ten bucks.

Turning to see if black hoodie has appeared—not so far—I dart from display to display, searching for sharp knives.

Part of me knows that if I'm afraid, I should call someone to pick me up. But I don't want to bring an innocent bystander into the mess.

As I rush down the Tangent aisle, I say a prayer to Saint Jude, patron saint of desperate cases and lost causes—I recite the prayer often, so know it by heart.

As soon as I say "amen," I find myself standing before a pegboard where packages of knives hang from metal rods. "Thank you, St. Jude," I say as I scan the display, searching for something in my price range. And, voila, there it is: a Chefmate 3-piece knife set for just $6.99.

I slide a package from the display, and as I turn into the main aisle, there he is—black hoodie, and he's using his phone to snap photos of me.

I hold the package of knives in front of my face and charge at the man—short, swarthy, and early twenties—knocking the cell phone from his hand and sending it skittering across the red and white tile floor. The man makes a dive for the phone, but since I'm three inches taller and twenty pounds heavier I block him with my shoulder and push him against the wall under the escalator.

While the man tries to regain his balance, I grab the phone and stick it in the back pocket of my slacks. Black hoodie springs toward me like a punch-drunk panther, grabbing me around the waist and trying to pull the pockets off of my pants.

The Tangent shoppers seem oblivious, immersed as they are in power shopping and bargain hunting—or maybe they don't want to get involved in a possible family squabble, lover's quarrel between a cougar and boy toy, or an altercation between a West Hollywood matron and her personal assistant.

As I continue to struggle with my stalker, I never once think of calling for help or screaming out. The entire day—from homeless Joyce and her request for a Marilyn Monroe photo, to Shelby Norris stiffing me for the exorbitant lunch bill, to Riley Taylor trying to scare me away from the writing gig for Milton, to this ninja stalker—has pushed me into an adrenaline-fueled rage.

I shove my opponent, stomp on his athletic shoes with the heels of my cowboy boots, kick his shins, and more—with only weak rejoinders from my bantamweight challenger.

"Ahh," I yell, finally finding my voice. "What the hell do you want?"

In response, the man yanks on my right back pocket with both hands, trying to get a grip on his cell phone.

"Why are you following me?" I scream.

Just then, a woman's voice calls out, "What's going on here?'

I don't turn from black hoodie—but, thanks to my acute peripheral vision, can see a tall woman dressed in a bright red vest, white shirt, and black pants.

I watch as the man turns his head toward the Tangent employee, then shifts his eyes to look at me. Reading the man is as easy as scanning a newspaper headline—he knows that whatever goes down, he'll be the loser. There is no way a young Latino can win any conflict against a middle-aged white woman. For him, the verdict will be guilty—no matter what the facts. I'd charged at him and had taken his phone. But the man will never convince anyone that he's the wronged party—instead, there will be a presumption of his guilt. I read all of this in the man's glance.

Black hoodie turns and sprints toward the exit, not worrying about the phone with its incriminating evidence of spying, not worrying about whoever hired him to follow me, not worrying about anything except getting back to Santa Monica Boulevard and running, running, running to the anonymous haven of undocumented Los Angeles, where he can become someone else and no one can ever connect him with this incident.

While the young man heads for the door, the Tangent employee fumbles with a phone attached to a support pillar, taking a half a minute before finally announcing in the weary, beaten-down voice of the corporate lifer, "Security, detain the man running toward the main exit. Security, detain the man running toward the main exit." She voices the statement with no more urgency that she would have used to announce a manager's special for athletic socks.

By the time the woman finishes the announcement, I feel certain that black hoodie is halfway back to East Hollywood, Boyle Heights, Pico-Union, or any of the other Latino enclaves where he can disappear.

"You all right?" the Tangent employee asks, and, before I can answer, adds, "Come with me."

The woman nods toward the vast void of the store, indicating somewhere and nowhere at the same time. I figure some corporate bureaucrat will ask me to file a report or even call the police.

As the Tangent employee marches like a corporate robot toward that big wherever, I turn and head for the door—careful not to run because I don't want to be mistaken for a thief. I duck in and out of clothing displays and up and down a blur of aisles until finally I'm at the door and then on the street. Anyway, what good would it do to file a report? It isn't as if I want the guy deported. Besides, after what happened tonight, I'm sure he'll never bother me again.

◀ ELEVEN ▶

Five minutes later, I'm in a cab heading for home—after convincing the driver to stop at an ATM so I can get cash for the fare, another expense added to an already expensive day. But there's no way I'm going to walk to 7000 Iceberg Street in the dark to pick up my car. The taxi is a few miles down the road before it dawns on me that I should have let the driver take me to Iceberg Street. I only hope my car will still be there—without a ticket—when I return tomorrow.

I love riding in cabs—I love it anytime somebody else drives, giving me a chance to sit back and take in the sights. The driver is taking the slow route across Sunset—because of the ATM stop—and Santa Monica Boulevard would be faster and cheaper, but I decide to enjoy the ride. It's a luxury I can't afford, but as long as I'm here, I may as well float on the current of nighttime L.A.

As we drive east, I turn and view the last strands of sunset through the back window. The cab is quiet –no radio, no chatter from the driver—just the buzz of the engine and the whistle of air through the windows. Outside, everything takes on a violet hue, as if all of life's bruisings and batterings have risen to the surface and will soon dissolve into the night. This is when I like L.A. best—and even feel I might love it—when the sun is about to set.

At sundown, I always feel a mixture of nostalgia, romance, regret, and hope—a sublime cocktail that I down with pleasure. Whatever I've gone through during the day—and on this day, it has been a lot—the bittersweet dusk makes it all worthwhile.

It's after eight and the sunlight is bowing out for the day— there are just a few more minutes to witness the glowing glory of it all. I float on the scene, the moving canvas appearing on the window, feeling good, feeling great, feeling all is right, very right, with the world.

My mellow groove dissolves in an instant. I feel a strong vibration and my first thought is . . . earthquake!

I clutch the seat in front of me and say to the driver—a middle-aged guy with a red toothpick protruding from his mouth—"Did you feel that?"

The driver shrugs and moves his toothpick from the right side to the left side of his mouth.

Another few seconds goes by before I understand that it isn't an earthquake—it's black hoodie's cell phone vibrating in my back pocket. Yes, the buzzing insistency of the world always comes calling when you're enjoying a transcendent moment. So much for the sunset.

I flip open the phone and see the text message: "Where in the hell are you?"

▼

When I drag through my front door, it seems like days since I left home at noon. It's dark in the apartment, except for a gray glow at the south-facing windows. I can see Lucy and Liam slinking toward me in the shadows, cowering, as if afraid of getting catnapped. Whenever I arrive home by means other than my own car, the cats act this way. I find it funny that they don't know it's me unless the rumblings of my 1998 Toyota precede my arrival.

"Liam, Lucy," I call out, but don't turn on a lamp. I drop my bag and with my last bit of energy trudge to the oasis of my favorite object in the world—the midcentury Herman Miller sofa, circa 1950, designed by the Eames, that by a miracle, I'd snagged for forty bucks at the mid-city Goodwill Store.

Ah, it feels so good to finally sit down in my apartment. I expect the cats to jump up beside me—I keep the prized sofa covered with a duvet when company isn't around, not that I have much company. It's one of my quirks that I don't like people, other than close friends or family members, to bring their vibes into the space where I work.

I glance outside, where the lit-up windows from the apartment across the way float like paintings of windows in the fading daylight.

Where are the cats? Where did they go? They always jump on the sofa and sit next to me when I get home. But I'm too worn out to look for them. I lean my head back and then everything goes dark.

▼

I wake up in darkness with sweat rolling into my eyes. I'd passed out from exhaustion before turning on a fan. My neck is stiff from sleeping in an upright position with my head tilted back. My mouth is dry and I have to use the bathroom, but there is something much more urgent.

"Liam! Lucy!" I call. How could I have fallen asleep without finding out where and why the cats are hiding?

I fumble for the lamp cord, but before reaching it, the phone I'd taken from black hoodie starts vibrating, causing the glass coffee table where I'd left it to clatter.

I pick up the phone and flip it open. A woman is yelling, screaming, and crying in Spanish—if you can cry in Spanish, and this woman can. I feel sorry for this wife, mother, girlfriend, or sister of black hoodie. I want to comfort the upset woman, but the only Spanish words I can remember at the moment are casa (home) and comida (food), probably I'm glad to be home and feel famished.

"Por favor! Por favor!" the woman wails. You could hear her yelling in the next room, which is probably why what happens next happens next.

A hand grabs the phone—and I make out the silhouette of a man in a hoodie. The man is a dark ghost, a blackened outline, and for a moment I wonder if I'm still asleep.

The shadowy hand grabs the phone, puts it to his ear, and starts yelling in Spanish at the woman on the other end. After a few exchanges—the only word I pick up is "nada"—the shadow walks to the window and lowers the blinds, then makes his way toward the other side of the room. I still haven't said a word. I know who this is and why he's here. I don't want to waste my time saying the obvious ("What are you doing here?" "Get out!" "I'm calling the cops!") and instead focus on how I'm going to handle this intruder.

The lamp snaps on, sending out a flash of light that strikes my eyes like the atomic blast at Los Alamos.

"Ah," I call out, covering my face with my hands. According to my ophthalmologist, my eyes have just ten percent of "normal" pigment. A sudden burst of light or direct sunlight—or even a bright computer screen—can send me into a reeling nausea and migraine that can last for hours.

I listen and hear what sounds like someone sitting in my brown naugahyde chair—a 1960s beauty that I'd purchased at a Salvation Army store for just two dollars and fifty cents. It's one of the few items of furniture I'd shipped when I'd moved to L.A. I don't allow anyone to sit in the chair—I don't even sit in it. On the other hand, the intruder is so skinny that the chair can probably hold his weight.

After taking some deep breaths to calm my stomach—churning from hunger and bright light overload—I stare at the intruder through the splayed fingers that still rest over my eyes.

I'm relieved that black hoodie doesn't have a black eye from our encounter at the Tangent Store. I'd started to feel remorse about the incident—until he showed up in my apartment. Now I envision how nice a big purple shiner would look on each of his eyes.

"You've got your phone," I say, taking my hands away from my face. "Now leave."

"Are you sure nothing else is missing?" he asks, with no trace of an accent.

"Who in the name of God are you and what in the name of God do you want?"

In answer, the man begins to unzip his black hoodie. Many possibilities pass through my mind, but the man finishes unzipping before my imagination gets very far. With a ceremonial flourish, he opens his jacket to reveal Milton Kingman's brown accordion folder.

"Unless you're armed, I know I can take you," I say.

Black hoodie laughs and keeps laughing. He doubles over, holding the accordion folder against his knees. I have no idea what's so funny. Wasn't I the victor during our encounter at Tangent? Didn't I wrestle away his phone and cause him to race out of the store?

His laughter tapers off and he lets out a big "ahhhh." He sits up straight, still smiling.

"I'll just warn you," he says, "don't try it at home."

"Who the hell are you and what the hell do you want?

"It's a long story and I'm starving," the man says. "Do you have anything to eat?"

◄ TWELVE ►

I give the intruder a choice of sandwiches—egg salad, tuna salad, salmon salad, peanut butter and jelly, or grilled cheese. I don't eat meat and don't keep much food in the apartment.

Black hoodie, who'd introduced himself as Ryan, sits at the dining table—which also serves as my main writing space—and drinks iced tea while he waits for his sandwich (grilled cheese).

I never allow anyone to sit at the place where I work—it's how I try to preserve my writing mojo. But when a thug breaks into your home and tells you he's about to steal some invaluable research material, you don't have much choice but to let him into your space.

I make a great grilled cheese—my favorite thing in the world to eat. I use organic wheat bread, unsalted butter, and organic cheddar. I know the precise moment to place the buttered bread into the heated skillet. I understand just how long to cook each side and the temperature that offers the best browning of the bread and melting of the cheese. I'm going to blow away this burglar with the sandwich. This is one of my major character flaws—I'm competitive and a showoff when it comes to anything I'm really good at.

While the sandwich sizzles in the skillet, I whip up a pot of tomato soup—made with salt-free tomato sauce, Greek yogurt, olive oil, a dash of celery salt, and a sprig of basil.

While I cook, I keep waiting for Ryan—a too-obvious fake alias for a Latino—to say something. I turn and see that he's sound asleep, sitting up straight, with his mouth hanging open, revealing a set of perfect teeth.

This is my chance to call 911. I flip the sandwich to the other side, put a lid on the soup, grab my cell phone, then slip into the bathroom.

I sit on the edge of the bathtub and dial 9, followed by 1, and then slam the phone shut.

I have to find out what this is all about—and if the cops arrest the would-be burglar, I may never know. I stuff the phone into the back pocket of my slacks and make my way back to the kitchen, where the grilled cheese sandwich and soup are ready. Ryan is still asleep in a sitting position at the dining table.

I place another sandwich into the skillet and stand at the stove eating the first one I'd prepared. Mmmmm, how I love grilled cheese sandwiches—a perfect remedy for anything that ails me.

The scent of butter and cheese finally lures Liam and Lucy from their hiding place—I assume the cats have been holed up inside the box springs (they'd clawed their way in from the bottom the day the bed had arrived from Sears).

I clip off a buttery corner of my sandwich for each of the cats, then crumble the bread and cheese onto small dishes. They slink into the kitchen, while keeping their eyes on the intruder—torn between fear and temptation. Butter wins out.

As I watch Ryan sleep like a silent corpse—I've never known a man who didn't snore in his sleep—I realize that in a way I envy him. He looks so relaxed, so comfortable, so at peace. How can someone sleep like that—and in a sitting position, no less?

I turn the sandwich in the skillet and take another bite of mine. The cats are sitting side by side on the sofa washing their faces in synchronized movements.

I'm starting to worry that something is wrong with the sleeping intruder—is it possible to die and remain in an upright position? I take a few steps closer, listening for the sound of his breathing. As I get within an inch of his face, he opens his eyes wide and says, "Sandwich ready?"

▼

As he eats his soup and sandwich, the intruder spins a tale so outlandish and outrageous that I figure it must be true. Ryan—which he insists is a his real name, explaining that for decades Mexican mothers have given their children Anglicized names to help them fit into the American mainstream—is a private detective. Someone hired him to follow me and steal the Milton Kingman file.

But Ryan is not just a private investigator—he runs a detective agency, with many operatives in his employ. Since the downturn in the construction industry, people aren't swinging into Home Depot to hire cheap labor. But many people in Hollywood seek out private investigators to follow a spouse or lover, check out a business rival, or conduct surveillance—and even the rich are looking for a cheap alternative to high-priced detectives. Ryan seized an opportunity and, after a few years in business, has tons of work—and employs many men and women who formerly worked as housekeepers, janitors, landscapers, and day laborers.

"The person who hired me to follow you," Ryan says, wiping his mouth with a napkin, "is one of my oldest clients, and one of the biggest pains. Not to mention one of the cheapest, most demanding a-holes I've come across. I can't stand the SOB."

I put my hands around my sweating glass of ice tea, feeling the coldness seep into me. I have no idea where this conversation is going. Why is Ryan revealing all this? Is it some kind of shakedown or setup?

"You're telling me this much," I say, "so I'm assuming you're going to tell me who it is."

Ryan takes a bite out of an oatmeal cookie. He chews and swallows as if mulling over his options before saying, "I wish I could."

My interviewing style is that if somebody won't answer one question, ask another—usually something unrelated to put the interviewee off-guard.

"How did you get in here tonight?" I say, wiping my hands on a dishtowel.

"Bedroom window. Just popped out the screen and popped in."

I live on the second floor and the only way into my bedroom window is with a ladder—or by climbing the stucco wall. But before I can ask anything else, he adds, "I was here when you got home."

"No way," I say.

"I had a car waiting outside Tangent. The driver brought me here."

"You took Santa Monica Boulevard."

"How else?" he says, rattling the ice cubes in his glass. I get the hint and pour him more iced tea from a pitcher.

"My cab driver took Sunset," I tell him.

"You shoulda said something. They do that to run up the fare."

"So why did you wait so long to reveal your royal presence?"

"Sarcasm, huh?"

"What took you so long?"

"I was hoping you'd come home, turn on the lights, and run right to the folder. That way I wouldn't have to look around for it."

"Were you feeling tired?" I ask. "Or are you just lazy?"

"I didn't see any reason to tear the place apart. I like to keep things in order when I can."

"And you didn't feel like wrecking the apartment, even after I'd beat the hell out of you at Tangent."

"You knew I couldn't defend myself. I didn't want to take a chance of getting arrested," he says. "Besides, I'd never hit a woman, especially somebody my mother's age."

My e-cigarette cartridge is empty, so I pop a piece of Nicorette in my mouth and chew. I'm really, really, really tempted to run to the convenience store at Franklin and Vermont and light up in the parking lot where all the homeless people congregate.

By the time Ryan finishes eating, it's almost ten o'clock. He stands up and says, "I gotta deliver the goods by midnight."

"That's not going to happen," I tell him, chomping on the Nicorette, not really caring if I look like a no-class, crass, crude, rude, gum chewer.

"After I get paid, I'll get somebody to steal it back."

"Why should I believe you?"

"Look, I have to deliver so I can stay on this freak's good

side. It'll be better for you, anyway. If I have the file, I won't need to follow you. You've been under surveillance for days. I'm surprised it took you so long to catch on."

"Who hired you to follow me? At least tell me that."

"I can't jeopardize this particular client's business. But I'm giving you my word. And I always keep my word. You'll get your file back by tomorrow."

"But if you steal it back, won't the person suspect you?"

Ryan shakes his head while he puts on his hoodie. "No reason to. This would be the first time it's ever happened. So why would the person think it's me? Besides, this individual has so many enemies—real or imagined—and is such a freaking fiesta of paranoia that there are hundreds of people to suspect before my name ever pops into this one's deranged mind. You wouldn't believe . . ."

Ryan stops speaking and looks toward the front door. I stare in the same direction. A key is turning in the lock and a moment later the door is creaking open.

I motion for Ryan to stay where he is, as I move to the front door. My perky, twenty-five-year-old neighbor Marelle stands in the entryway, and shrieks when she sees me.

"I didn't know you were here," Marelle sputters.

"You're some psychic," I say, never missing a chance to poke a hole in Marelle's claim to fame—she makes a living as a professional prognosticator, especially for stockbrokers.

"Your car wasn't in the lot."

"I took a cab home."

"I was going to bring over Lucy and Liam to visit with Patrick for a while. He seems depressed," she says.

Marelle and I have keys to each other's apartments in case we lock ourselves out or need someone to take care of our pets. Until now, I'd never realized that Marelle sometimes enters the apartment whenever she feels like borrowing my cats.

Ryan hasn't made a sound, but Marelle seems to detect his presence. Her eyes turn toward the dining area, which isn't visible from where she's standing.

"I've interrupted something," Marelle says. "I'm sorry."

"I'll bring over the cats in a little while," I tell her. "But I need you to do me a favor tomorrow."

"You want me to drive you to West Hollywood to pick up your car," Marelle says, then adds: "No problem."

After Marelle leaves, I trudge toward the kitchen. I can't wait to take a long bath and go to bed.

Ryan is holding Milton Kingman's file. He looks relaxed, refreshed, revitalized—he'd eaten, slept, and is now ready for another shift.

"How did she know you needed her to drive you to West Hollywood?" Ryan asks.

"She's a professional psychic."

"Can you get me her card?" he says. "In my line of work, I could use help like that."

▼

Ten minutes later, Ryan is gone—off to deliver the Milton Kingman file to his client.

After taking Liam and Lucy to Marelle—who'd insisted that the cats stay overnight—I run a bath and ease my tired bones in the tub with a frosty Heineken's at my fingertips. I've never felt more in need of a bath, a beer, and a nice long soak in Epsom Salt.

As soon as I submerge my body in the water and am about to bring the beer to my lips, my cell phone rings—as always, with the ringtone refrain from Bach's "Sleepers Awake." I consider not answering, but figure at this hour it might be a family emergency.

"Hello," I say into the phone, skipping my normal salutation.

"So how's my book coming along?"

I'm surprised that Milton Kingman stays up this late. It has to be nearly midnight.

"Well, Milton," I say, "considering that you gave me the job last Friday and this is the following Monday, I'd say I've made a great deal of progress."

"How many pages have you written?"

I want to tell him that it doesn't work that way. The writing comes at the end, after I've read and organized all the research materials and conducted interviews. But I know that's not what Milton wants to hear. He wants to see progress—he wants me to reassure him that the book is coming along. I hate to lie, but know that this particular client won't understand the truth.

"I'll have the book completed in less than eight weeks, Milton," I tell him in the low tones I usually use when trying to lure my cats from the box springs.

"How many pages have you written?"

I want to tell him that I can't start writing the book until I understand the story. But I know that he'll have no idea what I'm talking about.

"You're going to owe me that two thousand dollar bonus," I respond.

"But how many pages have you written?"

"Twenty," I respond.

"Good," Milton tells me. "We're making progress."

◀ THIRTEEN ▶

I spend the following morning doing Internet research on the movies Milton Kingman produced for Duke Galveston's company—most of them sci-fi and noir flicks made during the 1950s. After a few hours of checking and crosschecking, I have a list of five interview subjects—people who'd either appeared in the cast or worked on the crew. Shelby Norris—who'd told me she'd worked as a screenwriter—isn't mentioned anywhere, convincing me that she's an impostor.

Imdb.com lists actress Pauline Granton as appearing in three of the films and notes her birth year as 1930, making her well over eighty. The site also includes her husband's name, which I'm able to find at whitepages.com, along with a phone number.

I dial, get Pauline Granton on the line, tell her I'm writing a book about Duke Galveston and ask for an interview. The woman says she's free this afternoon at two and gives me her Bel Air address. It feels like I've just received a B12 shot in each arm. An interview with a woman who'd worked multiple times with Milton Kingman and Duke Galveston! Wow!

▼

When I crouch into Marelle's Mini Cooper, I start to say something, but Marelle answers "okay" before I even get the words out.

"So you know what I was going to ask," I say.

"I thought by now I'd convinced you of my psychic abilities," Marelle answers.

"Okay, then," I say.

"On the way," Marelle offers, as if reciting a memorized statement, "let's stop by Joyce's camp outside the Masonic Temple and see if she's there. You want to give her that picture of Elizabeth Taylor."

At least Marelle can't read all my thoughts.

When I see Joyce in her usual spot at Vermont and Franklin, I feel like letting out a Mormon-Tabernacle-Choir-worthy "Hallelujah." By turning over the photocopy of the Marilyn Monroe photo, I can free myself from the latest Joyce-related burden and embark on my day feeling lighter. I don't know why Joyce evokes such feelings of guilt and responsibility in me, but it seems that one way or another I'm always in the homeless woman's debt.

While Marelle double parks, I hop out of the car and hand Joyce the manila envelope

"Here you go," I say. "But, remember, you didn't get this from me."

"And why in the hell not?" Joyce says, hand on hip.

I sketch out what the clerk at the library had told me—that if someone sells a drawing based on the photo, it will amount to copyright infringement.

"You're freakin kiddin me," Joyce says, blowing dragonish blasts of smoke from her nostrils. "And who's going to enforce it? Who's going to stop me?" She stomps her foot so hard on the sidewalk that the heel of her flamingo pink stiletto breaks clean off.

I realize another tirade is coming and head back toward Marelle's car while Joyce curses and starts in on an impromptu shoe repair.

I'm not sure the reason, but something tells me to turn back and ask Joyce if she's ever met Shelby Norris.

As Joyce applies superglue to her heel, she says, "I need some details."

After I describe the woman—svelte, elderly, and elegant—and mention that I'd seen her at the Margaret Herrick Library the same day I'd run into Joyce outside the facility.

"Yeah," Joyce says, "I noticed her over there that day."

"Do you know her name?"

"No idea. But I saw her a few times in Beverly Hills. She puts on a good act, but she's homeless. We can always spot each other."

Homeless? That's the last thing that I'd have guessed. The woman had looked well groomed and très chic. How could she be homeless?

"What makes you say that?" I ask.

"I saw her run out on a couple of lunch checks. Restaurant people racing down the street after her."

"But she was so well dressed."

"And I'm not?"

"She was well dressed in a different way."

"Most of us get our clothes from the Goodwill box," Joyce advises. "You know, the stuff people leave outside before the store opens. This is L.A., honey. You can find some great threads that way."

▼

My trip to West Hollywood is the opposite of the previous night's cab ride—we're now traveling west in glaring daylight and the mood is not mellow. Marelle is doing me a favor, so I vow not to dictate which streets to take—even when the driver stays on Hollywood Blvd., the slow route past the Walk of Fame, where tourists, eyes to the ground, search for their favorite stars.

I'm relieved when Marelle makes a left on Vine Street— glad that she doesn't take the street all the way to LaBrea— avoiding Hollywood and Highland, one of the biggest tourist traps in the city, famous for the Chinese Theater and the superhero impersonators who charge tourists to pose for photos.

Silent during much of the ride—my thoughts on all the work I have to do on this particular day—I realize it's rude not to chat with someone going out of her way like this. Then I remember something I want to ask.

"There's this private detective who . . ." I say.

"I know," Marelle responds. The psychic seems to always know everything—maybe that's why I get weary of talking with her at all.

"Just this once, Marelle," I say, "humor me and act as if you don't know what I'm going to tell you."

Vine Street turns into Rossmore and the car starts to wind through a beautiful residential section of Hancock Park, filled with monumental old Hollywood homes.

"I want to live in one of these places someday," Marelle says.

"You mean you don't know if you will or you won't?" I ask.

"I can read for just about everybody except myself. You know that." Marelle sighs and adds, "So this private detective asked for my card."

"I'm going to see him later," I explain. "I can give it to him then."

Marelle opens her glove compartment and pulls out half a dozen business cards.

"What if he asks about your fee?"

"Tell him I'll give him a quote based on the assignment."

"Who knows," I say, "maybe you'll make tons of money solving cases for the detective and you'll be able to buy that fabulous home sooner rather than later."

"That's what I was thinking," Marelle says.

"So do you have any impressions about what kind of day I'm going to have?" I ask. After yesterday's nonstop debacle I could use some psychic insight.

"You know I don't do readings for free," Marelle says. "People don't respect something they don't have to pay for."

"How about a quid pro quo?"

"What are you offering?" Marelle asks.

"The continuing loan of my cats. You borrow them so often, I'm beginning to think you're using them as your psychic familiars," I tell her.

"You're going to meet with a man whose first name begins with the letter M," Marelle says.

"How about something I don't already know?"

▼

When Marelle drops me off in front of 7000 Iceberg Street, I'm relieved to find my car in front of the building, with no ticket on the windshield. I address St. Rita—patron saint of impossible cases—to thank her for this happy result. *"St. Rita, mystical rose of every virtue, my deepest appreciation."*

When I try to open the car door, the lock won't budge. It takes half a minute for me to remember that the driver's side door had jammed the previous day, and I need to get into the car from the passenger side. I'm just about to do that, when my head turns toward the building's entrance.

Here I am, I think, and when will I get back to this spot again? I check the time on my cell phone: 12:35. I have a few minutes to spare before taking off for Milton's place in Brentwood.

My curiosity won't let me leave the location without at least trying to get a glimpse inside Duke Galveston's former headquarters—site of the infamous 1974 break-in and robbery of confidential documents, including those related to the Watergate scandal. Duke Galveston's claim to fame is not only as a Hollywood mogul, but also as the largest government defense contractor and one of the world's richest men. Never before or since has there been a man as powerful, rich, famous, and mysterious as Duke Galveston.

I turn and bound up the walk as if I belong here—a trick I learned from a friend who lives in a dicey part of Hollywood and never has any problems, because she acts as if she owns the neighborhood. So with that attitude, I take big strides up the walkway and approach the front door, which breezes open when I push on it.

The foyer is high-ceilinged, hushed, and nearly church-like in its subdued aura. The art deco interior—1930s elegance, with streamlined accents—looks original, yet spruced up. I stand in one place and do a complete 360, taking small clockwise steps until I've viewed the entire room. And at the last step in my circle, I look up and there he is: Duke Galveston in a gigantic photographic portrait that measures over six feet high by four feet across—depicting the handsome Texan in his early twenties when he'd first come to Hollywood. It strikes me that the portrait is intended as life-sized.

I feel tears welling up in my eyes, as if I'm encountering the subject of my book in the flesh. It's the same feeling that came over me when I'd viewed Winged Victory and the Mona Lisa during my first visit to the Louvre. A personal encounter with an icon is like an out-of-body experience—you can't believe it's really happening and feel overwhelmed.

It isn't that I admire Duke Galveston or feel in awe of him—at this point, I still know very little about the man. No, it's the image of Duke Galveston, his standing and stature in the world as one of the most significant individuals in recorded history. I feel humbled to write about him, even if it's just a tiny part of his life story.

At the sound of footsteps coming down a hallway, I decide to head for the door before someone demands an explanation of why I'm here and what I'm doing—as if I knew.

◀ FOURTEEN ▶

I take Sunset to Milton's place in Brentwood and arrive at 1:15. It was a hot drive with no a/c, and I'd fanned myself with a U.S. Postal Service Priority envelope so I wouldn't end up soaked in sweat—not a good look for client meetings.

I park a half a block away and walk back. I didn't call ahead, so Milton isn't expecting me—I figured that with his increasing dementia he'd probably forget the appointment, and I don't want to take the chance he'll refuse to see me on short notice. I need him to sign a contract for my ghostwriting services—and if he balks at such a formal document, I have a simple letter of agreement as backup.

Milton hadn't shown any signs of decreased mental capacity the day I'd taken the job and received his check for four thousand dollars. But now that I see the bigger picture—Milton's memory challenges and a son who's trying to take over his assets—I need to protect myself by getting something in writing.

I start to ring the doorbell, but hear voices growing in volume behind the door, as if the people are moving closer to the front of the house. I put my ear to the door and listen. While I have sight challenges, my hearing is acute, well above average, especially in my left ear.

"I told you all I know," Milton says.

"One way or another I'm going to find out," Conrad shoots back.

Bark, bark, says Rudy, it seems, just to chime in.

"Let it rest, Conrad," Milton pleads. "Let it rest."

"How can I?" Conrad shouts. "I'm entitled to at least half the money."

"There's no way you can prove it. Please, Conrad, please quit tormenting me."

When I hear heavy footsteps clomping toward the door, I sidle off the porch and duck behind some bougainvillea bushes at the side of the house.

A moment later, Conrad squeezes out the front door, with Rudy trotting beside him. On the sidewalk, Conrad picks up

Rudy's leash and takes off running into the Santa Monica Mountains.

After I see Rudy round a corner, I tap a few times on Milton's door.

"Leave me alone! Please, Conrad, leave me alone," Milton mourns from inside.

"It's me. Dakota," I say in a voice just shy of a shout—a high enough volume for Milton to hear, but not loud enough for the neighborhood to know what I'm saying.

The door flings open and Milton waves me inside, then shuts the door.

"Do we have an appointment?" the old man asks. He's dressed as if going out to hit nine holes—visor, golf shirt, khaki pants, and Hush Puppies shoes.

"I didn't know you played golf," I remark.

"There's a lot you don't know about me," Milton says.

"Well, I'm waiting for you to tell me more."

"I told you everything I remember. You've got twenty pages. Write about two hundred more and we'll be all set."

"Milton, I forgot to have you sign a contract the last time I was here."

"Contract?"

"It just says that you hired me to write the book and promised to pay me four thousand dollars, with a two-thousand-dollar bonus if I finish in under eight weeks."

"Got a pen?"

▼

To reach Pauline Granton's address in Bel Air, I take Sunset to Sepulveda and drive north to Skirball Center Drive, an artery that turns into Mulholland Drive and takes me to the north gate of the pricey enclave.

Bel Air is the most exclusive area of Los Angeles—a location where only the wealthy, super-wealthy, and uber-wealthy can afford to live. In his heyday during the 1930s and 1940s, Duke Galveston owned numerous homes in Bel Air, saying he liked the area because it was close to the golf course.

Pauline Granton's house is somewhere down a narrow winding road crowded with the biggest trees I've seen in Los Angeles. I want to take a closer look at these magnificent specimens, but have to keep my eyes on the road—my challenged depth perception makes it difficult to gauge street widths, and I'm afraid of rolling off into a ditch.

I have the sensation I'm traveling through a Hansel and Gretel forest, and guess the area's planners intended it this way—the residents wishing to obscure their homes from anyone driving by.

I keep looking for address numbers to indicate where I am—a mailbox, a lamppost, something, anything—but realize I'm in an addressless void, an exclusive zone where the only way to get to your destination is to have been there before.

After driving up and down the road for a mile in either direction, I spot something large and yellow flashing through gaps in the foliage—and hope it isn't one of the mountain lions that live in the vicinity.

As I drive, I think about how much of L.A. is wild and untamed—bears, cougars, bobcats, deer, skunks, foxes, coyotes, plus mountains, canyons, the ocean, the desert, cacti, palm trees, redwoods, and on and on. Taken together, everything seems so surreal that it's hard to believe the area exists on planet Earth—especially so close to the L.A. megapolis.

I pull into a narrow pathway and drive beyond the trees and foliage until I spot a butter-yellow BMW that looks as if it might be older than my Toyota. On the phone, Pauline Granton had told me to keep and eye out for a yellow BMW, though I'm lucky to have found it on this unmarked road.

According to my cell phone, it's 1:14 and I'm sorry to be late, but feel certain that most people don't find Pauline Granton's address on the first pass.

I leave my car in the driveway—there's no way I can hide it by parking a few blocks away and walking back, since there are no curbs where you can park a car.

I make my way toward the ranch-style house set deep inside a grove of redwood trees. The place is small by Bel Air standards, but still an impressive piece of real estate—and I can't wait to view the inside.

I lift the brass ring on the lion's-head doorknocker and rap twice, the two clicks sounding like "tick tock." Yes, I have to keep track of the time so I'm ready when Ryan calls about returning Milton's research materials.

I hope Pauline isn't a stickler for punctuality. If she is, the interview will get off to an uncomfortable start or go nowhere at all.

A few seconds later, the door opens and a striking, petite woman—who looks as if she's in her fifties or sixties—greets me with a movie-star smile.

After apologizing for my tardiness, I introduce myself and the older woman holds out her hand and says, "I'm Pauline Granton."

She has the dramatic demeanor of a Golden Age of Hollywood star—ramrod straight posture, throaty voice, elegant hand gestures, and, most of all, that professional smile. This lady comes from the days when the studios sent actresses to finishing school, gave them elocution lessons, taught them how to dress and how to walk.

Pauline is well put-together, with a fresh manicure and perfect makeup—and, to my eye, the only thing that seems off is the woman's hair. It's just too thick and perfect—and I wonder if it's a wig.

I don't get a chance to check out the house because Pauline leads me through a hallway into a breakfast nook, a nice cozy spot for the interview. As I follow after the former actress, I watch how she moves, as if the very air is parting just for her to pass through. She is a star, still a star, and she comports herself as one.

"Have a seat," Pauline says, and I slide into one side of a leather booth.

"How much time do you have?"

Before Pauline can answer, a loud, prolonged groan comes from the other room, accompanied by what sounds like falling logs. Pauline doesn't flinch or even seem to blink, as if this happens all the time.

I hear a woman's voice say, "Everything's fine, Albert. Everything's fine."

The man behind the groan starts to moan, then transitions into a loud buzz and tapers off into a light hum.

I wait for Pauline to say something, but she seems oblivious to the noise—or just inured to it.

While I feel sorry for the poor man suffering from this affliction—probably Alzheimer's disease—I wonder if I'll be able to conduct an interview if this keeps up.

Well, just dive in, I tell myself.

While setting up my tape recorder, I ask some basic questions: does Pauline keep in touch with any other actors or crew members from the movies Duke Galveston produced, and does she have any photographs from those days—particularly does she have any photos of Duke Galveston?

"The answer is yes and yes," Pauline responds. "But let's do the interview before we get into that. I have at least an hour."

After some questions about Pauline's background and early days in Hollywood, I get to my major interest: Duke Galveston and Milton Kingman.

"You made five films with Duke and Milton during the 1950s, is that right?"

"I believe so," Pauline says. "Though it's hard to remember them. They were B movies, call them B minus."

"I understand that Duke wanted to capitalize on the UFO craze of the time with all these sci-fi movies," I say, hoping the statement will spark some commentary from Pauline.

"Duke just wanted a script with lots of parts for young women so he could feature a dozen or so of his girlfriends in the movie."

"So he lived up to his reputation," I say.

"Oh yes," Pauline says. "Duke was quite the Romeo."

From the other room, the man starts to shout: "Duke! Duke! Duke!" which sounds like Dooooookkkkk and some other words I can't make out.

"Yes, dear," Pauline calls into the other room, then turns to me. "My husband says Duke was a cheapskate."

"Was he?"

"Oh, yes," Pauline says. "Duke hated to pay anybody, which was maddening coming from a billionaire."

"So your husband worked for Duke as well?"

"Oh, yes," Pauline says. "He wrote a dozen screenplays for Duke."

▼

For over an hour, I interview Pauline Granton about her years working with Duke Galveston. Her answers are insightful, as if she's given the topic a great deal of thought over the years. In essence, she tells me that Duke was a charismatic, interesting, and creative person—but in many ways backward, unsophisticated, and simple.

"One thing above all you have to realize about Duke," Pauline says, running her finger around the edge of her jade bracelet.

I wait for a response while thinking how great Pauline looks for a woman in her eighties. She's bright-eyed, svelte, and dressed with impeccable taste in a Chinese black silk blouse and slacks. The former actress has style and class, plus a well modulated, cultured voice and graceful manner.

"And what's that?" I ask.

"It's strange," Pauline says. "And I don't know exactly how to put it."

I make a quick intake of breath, hoping and praying that Pauline will keep talking.

"I really don't know if I should say this," Pauline tells me, her voice trailing off.

I decide to wait, to not say anything for a moment. In cases like this, I've found it best to let the momentum of the person's words carry him or her forward. There's a streak in human nature that makes people want to spill their guts. Most people are just waiting for the opportunity, the opening, the question that will let it all come flooding out.

"Well," Pauline begins, "Duke was . . ."

At that moment, glass crashes in another room and a man shouts, "Duke! Duke! Duke!"

A woman calls, "Get back here, Albert."

The next thing I realize, someone is behind me, yanking on my hair. It seems that all hell has broken loose with scuffling and yelling. I put my hands to my head, trying to free myself from the pulling. Then the hands are gone.

"Ah," I hear the man cry, followed by the sound of a body thudding to the floor.

I jump up and turn to look. A tall, white-haired man is lying on an air mattress—as if it has appeared just for this purpose—and an African American woman dressed as a nurse is standing next to him with a hypodermic needle. In the man's hand is my hairclip, along with most of my hair. In his other hand is a pair of scissors.

I reach up and feel my hair—what's left of it. I figure this is probably why Pauline Granton wears a wig.

▼

An hour after my unceremonious scalping by Pauline Granton's elderly husband—a man suffering from Alzheimer's Disease who had no idea what he was doing—I'm sitting in the couple's dining room with photos spread before me on the table. The damage to my hair is now a fact of life—and I can do nothing about it at the moment. I refuse to even look in a mirror, but while sitting near the air conditioner feel a breeze on the back of my head for the first time in years.

Pauline has apologized over and over and offered the use of a scarf or hat—even modeling a few stylish numbers—but I'd declined. At this point, I'm more interested in getting what I've come for—information about Duke Galveston and Milton Kingman.

I feel sorry for Pauline. Apparently her husband can't remember anything in the present or recent past, but is doomed to relive all the horror, sci-fi, and noir scripts he'd written decades before. I figure my arrival had coincided with the horror phase of his recollections. Too bad he wasn't reliving a noir script—maybe he would have offered me a cigarette.

Turns out, Pauline is a packrat and has accumulated a researcher's treasure trove of material—stills from film shoots, candid photos, scripts, letters, cards, and more. And a contrite Pauline now gives me carte blanche to stay as long as I like—or come back as often as I want—to study the material.

I pick up a magnifying glass and examine the faces of the Venusian virgins in a still from a sci-fi flick Duke and Milton produced. I point at one of the starlets and hand the magnifying glass to Pauline.

"Do you remember her?"

Pauline puts her face close to the photo and says, "It looks like Shelly Morris."

Shelly Morris? I feel sure this is the woman now calling herself Shelby Norris.

"Were all these women Duke's girlfriends?"

"These and more. He set them up in houses and kept them under lock and key. When the thrill was gone, he took back the house."

"I met a woman yesterday," I begin, "who I'd bet is Shelly Morris."

"Shelly took it very hard when Duke cast her aside," Pauline says. "She even tried to sue him, saying he'd tricked her into sleeping with him."

"And how did he do that?"

"Apparently Duke took Shelly on a cruise and asked the ship's captain to marry them. As it turned out, Shelly was an eighteen-year-old virgin, and the captain was a fifty-year-old fake."

I don't know what to say. I try to imagine how the young girl had felt after such a breach and betrayal.

"That's what I was trying to get at before Albert attacked you," Pauline says. "Duke was a practical joker, a cruel one. He loved to feel he was putting something over on someone. But the odd thing was, Duke really had no sense of humor. It was just a mean streak, trying to get the best of people, trying to steal what was most precious to them."

Oh, Lord, I think. This is bad. There is nothing I dread more than learning that the subject of my book is a bona fide horrible person.

Duke Galveston had bought homes for a harem of women— and how many of them were now, like Shelly Morris, homeless?

"The sad part was," Pauline adds, "Shelly was really in love with Duke."

"I believe she still is," I say, remembering how Shelly had sparkled every time she'd mentioned Duke's name during lunch the previous day.

I feel Shelly's sadness seep into me and sit in silence for a few moments. Then I turn and look on the sideboard where banker's boxes are piled up.

"What's in there?" I ask, pointing to the boxes.

"Those are Albert's scripts and notes from when he worked for Duke," Pauline says. "I was getting ready to donate the files to one of the universities."

"I really need you not to do that right now," I tell her. "Okay?"

Pauline nods and a tear trickles down her still-smooth cheek.

"I just don't know what to do about Albert," she says. "You can't understand how hard it is to watch someone you love go through this."

Pauline puts her hands over her face and sobs.

"He was a good man," she says through her tears. "He was always such a good man."

I turn and put my hand on Pauline's shoulder to offer some comfort.

"I'm sure he still is," I say, not knowing if the statement has any meaning or even makes sense. How can a man be good— or bad—if he doesn't know what he's doing?

▼

Time challenged as I am, I don't know how many minutes or even hours I've spent in Pauline Granton's dining room sifting through memorabilia. Pauline divulges—acting sheepish about it—that she'd even bought some of the movie stills and publicity materials on eBay. It's one of her hobbies to follow on-line auctions for items related to "her" movies.

"It seems an odd thing to do, I know," Pauline says.

"Why is it odd?" I ask.

"It makes me seem like . . ." the actress stops, as if searching for the exact word. "Well, it makes me seem like the president of my own fan club."

I laugh, and Pauline's face registers shock and embarrassment—narrowed eyes and flushed cheeks.

Uh oh, I think. It's never good to laugh during interviews, even when something is funny. The interview subject can interpret a laugh in so many different ways—and never the way you intended.

"I wasn't laughing at you," I say in a matter-of-fact voice. It's not good to appear overly apologetic and fawning. Just state the truth. "I was laughing at myself because I think we all need to be presidents of our own fan clubs."

Even though we're two rooms away from the kitchen where Pauline's husband is passed out on the floor, I can hear him snoring. I'm tempted to reach up and feel the back of my head where the man whacked off my hair, but decide to stop at a Fantastic Sam's and get a cheap fix-it haircut on the way home.

As I'm reviewing a group of stills from a movie called *Alien Oracles*, my cell phone beeps with a text message. I pick up the phone and note the time: 5:32 p.m. The text message says: "Meet at James Dean statue Griffith Observ 7 tonight. R."

Since I never take the freeways because I'm afraid my old car will breaking down and I'll get stranded, it'll be a long haul back to the Eastside in rush hour traffic. I'll be lucky to make the seven p.m. appointment—and don't want to risk arriving late because it might be my only chance to retrieve Milton's file from Ryan. Well, no time for a visit to the hair salon.

When I read the text message my face must have registered concern because Pauline asks, "Is everything all right?"

"I have to meet someone across town at seven. It's important. I just hope I can make it on time."

"Where do you need to go?"

"Griffith Park."

Pauline smiles as if she has the perfect solution to the world's most difficult problem. Boy, these movie stars sure know how to beam, I think.

"Just take Mulholland Drive," Pauline says.

Mulholland Drive? The dreaded Mulholland Drive—the treacherous, winding road through the hills with dead man's curves and canyon drop-offs?

"I'm not a very good driver," I say, feeling this is a vast understatement.

"It's a beautiful road," Pauline says.

"I'm sure it is," I reply while gathering my things, "but I have an old car and it's not very road-worthy."

"I drive a 1977 BMW," Pauline says, "and I take Mulholland Drive all the time. I take it to the Hollywood Bowl for concerts at least once a week."

The Hollywood Bowl? That would mean that on her way home Pauline navigates Mulholland Drive in the dark on the outside lane with the canyons only inches away.

"I don't think I can take Mulholland Drive," I tell her. "It's too dangerous for me."

"Oh, come on," Pauline shoots back. "You owe it to yourself to experience Mulholland Drive at least once in your life. You're never going to have a better opportunity. You're here. Mulholland Drive is just a few blocks away. You'll be on the inside lane. And, best of all, you'll be in Hollywood in just thirty minutes."

I try to give Pauline a grateful smile—and I really am grateful. But there's no way in hell I'm taking Mulholland Drive.

◀ FIFTEEN ▶

It's 5:48 when I leave, and I hope and pray to reach the Griffith Observatory by seven. I'll need a miracle to get there in rush hour, and say a fervent prayer to St. Christopher for help avoiding heavy traffic and reaching my destination in a fast and safe manner.

After exiting through the Bel Air North Gate, I turn left on Skirball Center Drive and head toward Selpulveda, which I plan to take south to whichever east/west drag seems the safest bet for a getting across town asap.

But after a half block, I start to think about what Pauline had told me. Yes, this is the perfect opportunity to experience the scenic, albeit treacherous, Mulholland Drive. And what kind of life am I living if I just go through the motions, taking the long way around and letting my fears dictate my actions? Besides, I have a good reason to take Mulholland Drive—I can reach Hollywood in thirty minutes and arrive early for my appointment with Ryan.

I stop and make a left into a driveway and turn around. After a minute, I'm sailing down Mulholland Drive—and the road is as beautiful and scenic as everyone has told me. It's the ideal time of day for the drive, traveling east in the late afternoon with the sun behind me—the deep canyon to my left and the mountain wall on my right, the San Fernando Valley in the distance, the city shimmering in the smog.

But I can't really enjoy the sights. I have to keep my eyes on the two-lane road—and with my challenged depth perception, I need to give this my full attention.

I take a deep breath, telling myself the winding road isn't dangerous or daunting after all. But maybe that's because I'm driving below the speed limit. After just a few minutes, people are honking, urging me to go faster. I look in the rearview mirror to see who's laying on the horn and for the first time get a glimpse of the hatchet job that Pauline Granton's husband inflicted on me. The sight of my chopped hair makes me scream and swerve into the opposite lane, where drivers in oncoming cars blare their horns.

I manage to pull the Toyota back into my lane before crashing into oncoming traffic or tumbling into the canyon. But the cars are relentless, honking and honking and honking, so I try to speed up, but when I do, it feels as if the car has risen off the road and is floating above the asphalt.

Before me is a twisting curve, the canyon flickering with fog and highlighted with afternoon glints of sun that make it seem like the gate of hell.

My heart isn't beating anymore. It's on a pogo stick, leaping up and down and from side to side. I've never felt so terrified— and pray, now out loud, to get through this.

More honking and blaring horns, and I try not to look in the rearview mirror, but I have to—taking in the horrible sight of my mangled hair, plus the black SUV that's right up on my bumper. The road is clear on the other side. Why doesn't the driver just pass me? The vehicle moves even closer, right up on me, as if getting ready to push me off the road.

I remember what Ryan told me—that someone had hired him to follow me, and he's tailed me since the previous Friday, when I'd first visited Milton Kingman about the ghostwriting job.

Is someone following me now? Or is this just the way everybody operates vehicles on Mulholland Drive?

Praying nonstop, I drive for what seems like forever on the twisting, turning, treacherous, two-lane Mulholland Drive— with a black SUV on my tail the whole way. Every time I check the rearview mirror, I see multiple horrors—the horrific haircut from Pauline Granton's husband and the vehicle glued to my bumper.

I'm scared and shaking, and believe that only prayer and promises to be a better, kinder, more understanding person are keeping me from flying over the edge and tumbling into the canyons that border the road on the left or crashing into the mountainside on the right.

Without knowing I'm going to do it, I find myself making a sharp right turn at full speed onto Laurel Canyon Blvd.—and feel lucky that the car doesn't go into a spin. I don't know where the road leads—and, with minimal sense of direction, it takes me a minute to realize I'm traveling south.

Laurel Canyon Blvd. is a road through the hills, but without as many hairpin turns as Mulholland Drive. I keep driving, realizing I'm descending from the mountains. Soon, I end up in more traffic and encounter a red light. I gulp air and continue to pray, hanging onto the steering wheel, trying to get my heart back to a normal speed.

And then I arrive at Sunset Boulevard and know where I am and how to get home on this straight shot back to Hollywood. Hallelujah! I make a left onto Sunset and feel elated that I'm in familiar territory. I see the famed Chateau Marmont in the rearview mirror. The traffic is still heavy, but I should be able to make it to the Griffith Observatory by seven.

Thanks to my erratic driving, I've managed to shake the black SUV that's been following me.

▼

After taking a variety of shortcuts, I'm back in my neighborhood by 6:50. I turn left onto Vermont Avenue, then cross Los Feliz Boulevard, and make my way into Griffith Park and up the winding hill to the Griffith Observatory—memorialized in the 1955 film *Rebel Without a Cause* starring James Dean. The spot is so equated with Dean that a bust of the actor now greets visitors on one of the observation decks, which offer a panoramic view of L.A. and its environs.

I still feel shaky from driving on Mulholland Drive and not ready for another cruise into the hills on narrow winding roads, but what choice do I have? If I hadn't been so distracted at Pauline Granton's house, I might have sent Ryan a return text asking for a different meeting place at a later time.

Instead, I'd taken the path of least resistance, always a bad move for me—because the easy road usually comes with pitfalls in one form or another. In this case, another drive through the mountains, and if the meeting lasts longer than an hour, I'll have to travel down the winding road in the dark—a path nearly as daunting as Mulholland Drive.

Now that I have time to think for the first time all day, I wonder why Ryan wants to meet at the Griffith Observatory. He'd spent hours at my place the previous day. Why not just meet there?

I see the Griffith Observatory looming in the distance—as imposing and majestic as the Panthenon. This is where people come to look at the sunsets, the stars, the planets. It's where you go to get inspired, to feel the manifest destiny of living in California.

As usual during the summer, the Griffith Observatory parking lot is packed, and I have to follow people to their cars, hoping someone will back out and I can slip into the spot. Nothing is ever easy. God if I weren't running on sheer adrenaline, I'd pass out from anxiety and exhaustion.

At 7:05, I find a parking space, and start to get out of the car when I remember my hair. I try to get a glimpse of myself in the rearview mirror. There's no way I can meet with anyone looking like this. I glance around the car for a scarf and reach under the seats searching for a beret left over from the cooler months.

In the glove compartment, I find one of the scarves I'd bought years before for five francs in Paris—a tiger print in shades of green. I offer up a prayer to St. Genesius, patron of the theater—because this scarf is going to serve as my costume for the evening. I don't know how to tie scarves or even how to wear them, but try my best to drape this one around my head in a gypsy configuration, then knot it in the back.

At 7:08, I race through the parking lot and head toward the James Dean bust. I see a man standing with the fading sun behind him, his outline traced in purple and black, as if he's a figure in stained glass. It isn't Ryan, but as I get closer, I recognize who it is.

"You look surprised to see me," the man calls out.

"Do I?" I reply.

"I want to explain why I took off yesterday," says Riley Taylor.

It dawns on me that the text message had been signed "R," which I'd assumed stood for Ryan—since the detective is the only person I've planned to meet this evening.

The observation deck is crowded with people enjoying the approaching dusk. L.A. never looks more appealing than during a summer sunset. The day's heat has burned away and in the hills it's even chilly. I wish I'd worn a jacket over my black silk blouse.

"Let's walk," Riley says. I assume he wants to keep moving because it's difficult to conduct a private conversation with so many people milling around.

I tag along beside him as he strolls to the far end of the observation deck.

"I almost didn't recognize you in that scarf," he says.

"Bad hair day," I reply in a decided understatement.

When we're about ten feet from other visitors, Riley looks down at me and whispers, "I need the Kingman file."

"I thought I made myself clear yesterday," I tell him.

"I'm doing you a favor by warning you off the project," he says.

"And why are you so hell-bent on writing about this?"

Riley starts to say something, then stops. His eyes grow larger, then narrow, as if he's a camera trying to get his thoughts into focus.

"It's a big story, one of the biggest," he says after a thirty-second pause. "It's beyond you, Dakota. You write comic novels, romantic comedy screenplays, and celebrity memoirs. Why would you want to get mixed up in something that amounts to one of the biggest conspiracies every perpetrated on the public?"

"I didn't realize you knew that much about my work."

"I glanced at your website."

"I've written a few dramatic screenplays and some serious nonfiction books."

"You're trying to be funny, even now—when I've told you how serious this is."

"If this is why you called me up here, my answer is no. I've had a very long day, and I'm going home."

Before I can turn away, he grabs my arm and says, "You'll leave when I say you can leave."

I push Riley's hand from my arm and say, "Don't try that again."

I take a step back and he holds up his hands. "Look," he says, "I'm not trying to threaten you. I'm just warning you to drop the Kingman book before it's too late."

"Too late for what?"

"Before you learn too much and become a target."

"You talk in circles, and I've heard enough."

I head toward the parking lot. Riley trots a step behind me. After a moment, he says, "Aren't you curious? Aren't you curious at all, Dakota?"

His voice sounds smooth and velvety, the voice of temptation, of seduction, of serving up the one thing that can possibly change my mind.

I turn and face him. We're standing in a grassy patch near the Astronomers Monument.

"I've sworn off curiosity for today."

"I doubt that," he says. "I know you. I know what drives you. I know why you do what you do. I know why you put up with all the hassle and the headaches and the anxiety—because you want to know. You want to know every effing thing there is to know. Isn't that right, Dakota?"

It seems that a curtain has fallen and the day has come to a crashing halt. All of a sudden it's dark, dark night, with no hint of color in the sky. The sun has set—gone like a disappearing act, sudden and final.

"And I know you," I respond. "I know what drives you. I know why you do what you do. You're a thief and a vulture and a vampire—a barnacle attaching yourself to other people's work, other people's ideas, other people's ambitions. You don't have any thoughts of your own, so you have to leech off someone else. I pity you."

I start to run toward my car. I hear Riley running behind me, but don't cry out—unwilling to give him the satisfaction of believing he's frightened or intimidated me.

He catches up with me as I'm putting my key in the lock, and stands in front of the door, refusing to move.

"We've wasted a lot of time here tonight," he says, "without even looking up at the sky, and that's really what this is all about."

"Please step away from my car," I say.

"Not before I tell you why you have to give me the Kingman file."

"I don't want to hear anything you have to say."

"Yes you do. You're dying to hear what I have to say. Your curiosity is killing you."

Riley's right. I'm curious to know what his story is all about. What would drive someone to pursue something with such vehemence?

"How do you think Duke Galveston became the biggest government contractor in the country?" Riley asks.

I have no intention of playing along. If Riley wants to share his story, so be it. But there's no way in hell I'm going to answer any questions. He pauses, waiting for me to answer while gazing overhead as if expecting a comet to appear.

I'm trembling, not out of fear—out of cold. It's hard to believe that such a hot day has turned so chilly. Riley takes his eyes away from the sky long enough to notice my discomfort and starts to remove his suit jacket, but I put out my hand and say, "Please, we're not in a 1940s movie."

I unlock my trunk and rummage around in the jumble of stuff until I find the small quilt I use during visits to Venice Beach. After shaking out the sand, I wrap it around myself. Oh, a warm blanket feels so great when you're cold. For a minute, I don't even mind that this obsessive writer is holding me captive—not allowing me to leave until he's spilled his story. Well, speed it up, I want to say.

When Riley sees me wrap the blanket around myself, he says, "Now we're in a 1960s movie. *Beach Blanket Bingo*, for one."

"Never saw it," I say.

"Well I take it you've seen the movies Duke Galveston and Milton Kingman made during the fifties. Their schlocky horror movies. Their silly sci-fi flicks. Their Grade-C crime films."

"Get it in your head," I say, "I'm not answering any of your questions. So can I go now?"

"Not until I make you understand why you have to give me those research materials."

My stomach starts to roar. When and what did I last eat?

"You've got to listen to what I have to tell you," Riley says.

"Then I hope you're at least serving popcorn."

What time is it anyway? I figure the Griffith Observatory must have a closing time, but have no idea what it is. There are still plenty of people on the grounds gazing up at the stars and the planets, and most don't look in a hurry to leave.

I can't believe how cold I feel. Not that I really mind the cold, if I'm dressed for it. But I'm not. I'm wrapped in a blanket but still shivering.

"This is crazy," Riley says. "Why don't we at least sit in your car while I tell you the rest of the story?"

"Sorry," I say, "I don't know you that well." I pull the blanket over the top of my head, so I'm peeking at him from a window.

"How about meeting me at the House of Pies for coffee? We can finish up there," he says.

"I'm tired and I want to go home," I tell him.

"I can't rush this," he says. "There's a lot I need to explain."

"Look," I say, "I get it. You've developed some theories about Duke Galveston. Based on what you've said and what I've read in other places, I think I can guess your basic premise."

"I doubt that."

"Let me give you the short version because, as I've said, I'm cold, I'm tired, I'm hungry, and I want to go home."

"Fire away," Riley replies.

"Okay," I say, "here goes. During the 1930s and 1940s, Duke Galveston was the most famous aviator in the world. The government sought his advice about anything related to aviation."

I stop and look up at Riley, whose arms are folded across his chest—not showing resistance in his body language, but because it's getting colder by the minute.

"Keep going," he says.

"In 1947, when the UFO crashed at Roswell, New Mexico, the government called in Duke and asked him to take a look at the craft and the alien bodies. Later, his company won huge contracts to reverse engineer technologies found aboard the vessel."

I can't make out Riley's face in the darkness, but I hear clicking—as of he has TMJD and his jaw is popping.

"Since Duke was privy to so many secrets," I go on, "he basically blackmailed the government into giving him more and more contracts."

I stop and stare at Riley.

"Is that all?" he asks.

"Hell, no," I say.

"Go on," he says.

"The biggest mind-freak of all is that Duke produced his sci-fi movies under secret government contracts. The government needed to introduce the idea that we are not alone in the universe, and what better way to get the information into the public mind than through a Hollywood movie?"

"There's no way you could have known this," Riley says, "unless you stole my files or hacked my computer."

I hope Riley is kidding, but know he isn't. I realize it was a stupid showoff move on my part to spout out his conspiracy theories like this. Why wouldn't he think I'd breached his files?

"You must know," I say, "that these theories are nothing new. People have been saying this stuff about Duke Galveston for years."

"Where?"

"Good, God," I say, "didn't you even do a basic Google search before you cooked up all this in your mind?"

"But the Kingman file," Riley says, "has information that has never been reported. There are patent applications for inventions. Photos of the aliens, those that survived the crash. That material will take this from speculation to fact. Someone has to tell the story of how the government has been hiding information about UFOs from the American public for nearly seventy years. We have a right to know."

I'm tempted to tell Riley that I think these theories about Duke Galveston are sheer bunk, but don't believe it will do any good.

"And what are *your* theories?" Riley asks.

"You'll have to read Milton Kingman's book when it comes out."

"So that's it?" he says. "You don't have any questions for me at all?"

"Well, you were going to explain why you ran off yesterday at the wine bar."

"I forgot an appointment. It was urgent. I was late."

Before I can respond, I see a yellow flash in my peripheral vision and turn. On the crest of the hill stands the famous Griffith Park mountain lion, beautiful and majestic in the moonlight.

Riley turns to see where I'm looking. He jumps straight up about a foot, then runs into the darkness of the parking lot.

What a pussy, I think. And I'm not talking about the cat.

◀ SIXTEEN ▶

I'm relieved that this long, arduous, tortuous day is almost over as I head down the Griffith Park hill toward home. I'm too tired to even feel afraid driving a winding road in the dark. I turn on the radio and listen to a Bach violin concerto on KUSC-FM, finding a groove and feeling good that I'm on my way to food and tea and a nice comfortable bed.

A few minutes later, when I turn onto my street, I notice a police car parked in front of my building's entrance. I hope it's not another car break-in or that the obsessive woman on the first floor hasn't again called 911 because the building manager watered the lawn at a prohibited time.

When I park my car, I don't spot any police officers, and don't see any when I let myself into the courtyard. I figure the police are probably at another building.

I wonder what time it is. It must be at least nine, I tell myself. I'm ravenous and can't wait to dive into the pasta salad I'd made before leaving this morning.

As soon as I let myself into the apartment and before I can set down my bags or greet my cats, there's a knock at the door.

"Open up," a man's voice says. "Police."

I wonder if it's a scam—many robberies and home invasions happen when people open the door to this command. I look out the peephole and see Officers Flynn and Sanchez, the duo who'd investigated when Marelle's car was broken into the week before.

I figure they might want to ask more questions about any suspicious people I've seen in the area.

I set down my bag and open the door.

"Dakota Donovan?" Officer Flynn asks.

"Yes," I reply.

"You'll have to come with us."

"Come with you where?"

"To the station."

"Why?"

"To answer some questions."

"What kind of questions?"

"You'll find out at the station."

"At least give me some kind of reason."

"A complaint has been filed against you," Officer Sanchez says.

"For what?"

But the officer refuses to answer. He moves his hand in an ushering gesture and says, "Come this way."

During the twenty-minute ride in the back of the patrol car, I try to figure out who could have filed a complaint against me. A disgruntled client? A business acquaintance? A neighbor? The only thing that comes to mind is my lack of depth perception—maybe I'd sideswiped someone while the radio was blasting and hadn't noticed.

Whatever it is, I'm sure some kind of outrageous fee will be involved. At the rate I'm going, the four grand Milton paid me in advance to write his book will be gone by the end of the month—and how will I pay September's rent?

As the police car pulls into the parking lot at the LAPD station in Hollywood, I hope the officers won't ask me to remove my scarf—and I can keep my shorn head under wraps.

When we enter the station, I glance at the big round clock on the wall. It's 8:55 p.m.—and I'm exhausted and starving. Whatever this is all about, I hope I can clear it up and get out of here. I'm close to passing out.

The officers lead the way into what looks like a conference room and instruct me to sit down. When I comply, Officer Flynn, a redhead in her forties, refers to a report attached to a clipboard and summarizes the charges. Conrad Kingman has accused me of grand larceny and elder abuse, stating that I'd obtained four thousand dollars from Milton Kingman, his father, under false pretenses, and had taken advantage of a man suffering from dementia.

The officer produces a photocopy of Milton's canceled check.

"How do you respond to these charges?" Officer Flynn asks.

"May I show you something from my bag?" I respond.

Officer Sanchez retrieves the bag from the front desk, and, with a few instructions, I explain where to find the contract Milton signed.

"I'm an established ghostwriter," I state. "I can provide any number of references."

"So Mr. Kingman hired you to write a book for him?"

"That's right."

"His son says Mr. Kingman is incapable of making those kinds of decisions due to his diminished mental capacity."

"As far as I know, Milton Kingman is in charge of his business affairs and has not been deemed incompetent by any court. I took on this project in good faith and have been working diligently on the book since I accepted the assignment last Friday."

The officer studies me for a moment, then responds, "Conrad Kingman says his father doesn't remember hiring you to write a book."

"There's some kind of conflict between the father and son," I explain. "Mr. Kingman told me his son is trying to take over his assets and is stealing items from his home. I don't want to get in the middle of this. Then again, I shouldn't be penalized for accepting a project in good faith and moving forward with that assignment."

"It says in your contract that Mr. Kingman will pay you four thousand dollars to write the book."

"That's right. It's much lower than my usual fee, but I made an exception because I had some open time in my schedule."

"Do you always get paid in advance?"

"Not always. But that's what Mr. Kingman wanted to do."

"Wait here for a minute," Officer Flynn says, then stands up and leaves the room.

While she's gone, I have to pinch myself to stay awake. I'll look like a cavalier criminal if the officer returns and I'm asleep.

When I glance up, Milton Kingman and his son are standing in the doorway next to Officer Flynn.

I know Conrad brought his father to the police station to prove that Milton doesn't recognize me. And in my green tiger-striped headscarf, he might not be able to recall who I am. But I'm still not ready to take off the scarf and reveal the hair hacking Pauline's husband gave me.

Instead, I try another tactic. "Four thousand bucks," I say.

"Dakota," Milton replies, "I almost didn't recognize you in that scarf."

The police officers look from Milton to me and then to Conrad, whose downturned mouth makes him look like a sad Muppet.

Officer Flynn points at me and says, "Take off the scarf."

"If you don't mind, I'd rather not," I say.

"Catch a cold?" Milton asks, taking a seat at the other end of the table.

Should I make something up or tell what happened? I realize it'll be easier to just state the facts.

"I went to Bel Air today to interview Pauline Granton . . ."

"Oh, how is she?" Milton asks.

"Fine. Lovely woman," I say.

"Oh yes," Milton croons, eyes twinkling.

"Take off the scarf," the officer repeats.

I untie the scarf and pull it off my head with a dramatic flourish. The two officers and the two Kingmans gasp when they see my hair.

"What happened to you?" Milton whispers, as if overcome with shock.

"While I was interviewing Pauline, her husband came up behind me and hacked off my hair."

"Her husband? You mean Albert?"

"He has Alzheimer's and is reliving some of the horror scripts he wrote for you and Duke."

"What were you doing out there?" Milton asks.

"Trying to get additional material for your book. Pauline has boxes full of photos, scripts, and other items. She's even accumulated memorabilia by purchasing items on eBay."

Milton turns to Conrad, who averts his eyes, pretending to stare at the law enforcement poster tacked to a bulletin board.

Milton pounds his fist on the table. "Officers, I want you to arrest my son. He's been stealing my belongings for years and selling them on eBay. Good God," he says, "Pauline probably purchased my stuff from Conrad. It's mine and I want it back!"

The LAPD officers tell Milton he'll have to provide evidence of theft before they can arrest his son for stealing his belongings. They explain that Milton will have a difficult time proving the case, because Conrad can say that his father gave him the items in question.

While Milton discusses the situation with the police officers, Conrad stands hunched over at the side of the room, eyes like slits—a cornered animal plotting his next move.

It's now nearly ten at night. I wonder how long this is going to take—and whether the cops intend to drive me home or if I'll have to put up the money for a cab ride.

Officer Flynn picks up my contract for ghostwriting Milton's book and shows Milton the last page.

"Is this your signature?"

Milton takes his reading glasses from the inside pocket of his suit jacket and puts them on. He glances at the document.

"Yes, that's my signature."

As if he's just thought of something, Conrad lets out what sounds like a seal's bark, and shoots out, "When did you sign it?"

Uh-oh, I think. Is Conrad going to make a point out of my taking the four thousand dollar check the previous Friday and asking Milton to sign the contract this morning? I'd predated the contract so it would agree with the date of the check, but didn't ask Milton to put down a date when he'd signed.

Milton hesitates for a moment, then looks at me. I think I see him wink.

"I signed it the same day I gave Dakota the check," he says. "Last Friday."

I don't see any point in refuting Milton. After all, what difference does it make to anyone other than Conrad?

Officer Sanchez, a man in his late twenties with knit sleeves pulled over what I figure are tattoos, asks Milton, "Is there any reason you paid for the project in advance?"

Milton leans back in his chair and rolls his eyes toward the ceiling. He seems to be enjoying the attention.

"Well, Officer," Milton begins, "Dakota said I could give her a down payment of twenty-five percent. But I decided to pay upfront because my son has been trying to get his greedy paws on all my money. I wanted to make sure I paid for the project in its entirety before anything happened. My son has nothing better to do than to spend his days plotting how to torment me and rob me blind."

Officer Sanchez turns to Conrad and says, "What do you have to say for yourself?"

Conrad gazes at a spot over the officer's shoulder and clamps his mouth shut.

Sanchez's partner Flynn stares at Conrad and says, "You have wasted a lot of people's time tonight. Mr. Kingman. You have wasted the resources of the LAPD. You may be subject to a fine related to a nuisance complaint. You will hear from us."

Conrad turns to Milton and says, "Come on, Dad. Let's go."

He walks over to Milton and tries to raise him up by his elbow. But Milton shrugs him off.

"Unhand me," Milton says. "And as these people are my witnesses, you will not derive one penny from my estate. I am giving everything to charity."

Conrad's face arranges itself into a slow-motion sinister smile. He says, "Good luck with that, Dad. If Conrad Hilton couldn't get away with it, neither will you."

I know Conrad is referring to the hotel magnate leaving his fortune to Catholic charities—and his children suing for the money. The Hilton offspring won the case—proving that it's hard to disinherit your kids, even if they are, as Milton put it, robbing you blind.

Rather than wait for Milton to respond, Conrad turns and pushes his giant body through the door—and, I figure, out of the building.

"Guess you'll have to drive me home, Dakota," Milton says.

◀ SEVENTEEN ▶

Since I don't have my car, I can't give Milton a ride from the police station in Hollywood to his home in Brentwood. He asks if I'll accompany him to his house in a cab so we can discuss the book's progress, and he'll pay for the taxi to take me back to Los Feliz.

I agree, but tell him the cab will have to stop on the way so I can grab something to eat during the ride. It's now nearly eleven p.m., and I know I'll be lucky to find anyplace open. Unlike New York and Chicago, L.A. goes to bed early, with very little nightlife during the weekdays—probably because it's basically a one-industry town where people have to get up with the sun.

I direct the cab driver to stop at a 7-Eleven near Sunset and Highland. I ask Milton if he wants anything, but he says no. I grab a cup of coffee, a package of Lorna Doone cookies, a bag of Sun Chips, and a container of blueberry yogurt.

I advise the cab driver to take the streets to Milton's place, because it will give us more time to talk about the book. During the ride, Milton sits next to me holding his silver-tipped cane and gazing out the window, as if he's an emperor surveying his domain.

While I eat my snacks, Milton relates stories from his life. I'm amazed that he's opening up like this—because just a few days ago he'd said there was nothing more to share.

When Milton reaches the chronological point in his tale where he meets Duke Galveston, I ask a question for the first time since he'd started talking.

"How did you meet?"

"Albert Simms introduced us. He and Duke were best friends."

"Pauline Granton's husband?"

"Right. Albert and I were in the same Army unit during the war. He got me my start in the picture business."

"And how did Albert and Duke meet?"

"They were both aviators. They met at one of the airfields."

If only Albert didn't have Alzheimer's, I think. Now that would be an interview—everything I've always wanted to know about Duke Galveston.

I remember the photos I'd seen at Pauline's house—stills from some of the movies Milton and Duke produced.

"Do you remember a woman named Shelly Morris?"

"Oh, yes. She and Duke were involved for quite some time. I used to work with Duke on some of the inventions at their home in Bel Air."

That's just what Shelly Morris—calling herself Shelby Norris—had told me during our lunch.

"Duke and Albert used to go after the same women," Milton says. "It was like a competition with them."

"Pauline told me that Duke hired a harem of his girlfriends to appear in many of your movies."

"That's right. Geraldine was in that group. I believe she dated both Duke and Albert before she ended up with me."

I wonder if I should bring up the delicate subject of Conrad's paternity. Based on the conversation I'd overheard this morning, Conrad is trying to learn the identity of his biological father.

And then it dawns on me—Conrad thinks he's the biological son of Duke Galveston, and wants to sue for a portion of the multi-billion-dollar estate. Maybe that's why he's buying and selling Duke Galveston memorabilia on eBay—he's trying to get his hands on an item that contains Duke Galveston's DNA.

▼

When the cab pulls in front of Milton's house, I help my elderly client out of the vehicle and escort him to his front door. I wait while he turns the lock and clicks on a light inside the house. He turns to me and says, "Well, here's looking at you kid," the line Humphrey Bogart utters to Ingrid Bergman at the end of *Casablanca*.

The more I get to know Milton, the more I realize that he views himself as a romantic hero—and I'll make sure he comes across that way in the book.

"And here's looking back at you," I respond.

Milton seems pleased with the remark and even lets out a short laugh. He reaches in his pocket and pulls some bills, which he slips into my hand.

"For the cab and your expenses to date," he says.

I decide not to look at the money until I'm back in the cab. If he gave me too much, I'll return it next time I see him, and if it's too little, I'll make up the difference.

Milton takes a deep breath, his chest visibly inflating. "I guess we showed Conrad," he says.

I don't like getting lumped into this "we." I have no quarrel with Conrad—in fact, I hope that he and Milton can resolve their differences. My only gripe against Kingman the younger is his false accusation that I'd conned his father out of four thousand dollars—and feel lucky that I'd had the foresight to get Milton's signature on the contract earlier in the day.

"I don't like family feuds," I say.

"He's never warmed up to me as a father."

I wonder whether to ask the question I want to ask. The timing seems perfect—other than the waiting cab—and the situation may not present itself again.

"Forgive me if I'm overstepping my position," I begin, "but does Conrad think Duke Galveston is his father?"

Milton clears his throat, then waits a few moments before responding.

"For over twenty years, Conrad tried to get the answer out of Geraldine. But she would never budge. She'd always respond with something like 'Milton Kingman gave you his name. Milton Kingman raised you. Milton Kingman supported you. Milton Kingman is your father.'"

"And how did Conrad react?"

"I always felt he didn't like me. We just never clicked. That's one of the reasons he's spent decades trying to learn the identity of his biological father."

"Who do you think that is, Milton?"

"There are several candidates. I never pushed the issue with Geraldine. We were happy together, so why bring up the past?"

▼

As the cab heads back to Los Feliz, I reach in my bag for my cell phone to check the time. When I can't find the phone, I figure I must have left it in my car.

"Is it after midnight?" I ask the driver, an African American man in his fifties.

"Just about," he says. "Mind if I play some music?"

"Feel free."

And soon we're cruising to Miles Davis's *Kind of Blue*, one of my favorite albums. I slip into a mellow groove, zooming across Sunset, letting my mind drift and taking in the nighttime sights and sounds of L.A.

I'm lucky that neither Conrad nor Milton asked the where-abouts of the confidential folder. Where did I put Ryan's phone number? Why didn't I contact him about the drop-off? What am I going to do if he doesn't return the material?

It feels as if I've been working on Milton Kingman's book for years—and it hasn't even been a week since I took the job.

As I see it, there are several ways to approach the book. Milton hired me to write an exposé—all about his and Duke Galveston's encounters with UFOs, aliens, and alien technologies. This is the basic premise of what Riley Taylor intends to write—expanded into a more wide-ranging conspiracy. But that's not the book I want to ghostwrite.

I prefer to focus on Milton's rags-to-riches tale—from poor no-body to prolific Hollywood producer. Milton was one of the B-movie kings of the 1950s, and an insider's look at the business during this era would serve as an appealing way to tell his life story.

Besides, something Pauline Granton said makes me doubt the conspiracy line of thinking. I wouldn't put it past Duke Galveston to have created his own myth.

▼

When I step into my apartment, I smell cooking—eggs, toast, and coffee. The cats don't greet me at the door. Before I can figure out my next move, Ryan is standing six feet away with a spatula in his hand.

"Thought you wouldn't mind if I had something to eat while I waited," he says.

"I hope you made enough for two," I tell him.

"Take off your scarf and stay awhile," Ryan says.

"If you don't mind, I'd rather leave it on," I respond.

▼

Thirty minutes later, Ryan is clearing the plates and washing the dishes.

"Leave them," I say.

"I'll feel better if I clean up," Ryan replies.

"Do you have OCD?" I ask.

"I like things neat," he says. "It's just the way I am."

"I guess I'll have to get you a key," I tell him. "I can't have you climbing in windows or picking my lock."

"Marelle let me in."

"Why would she do that without asking me?"

"She's psychic, so she knew it would be okay to let me in."

"So are you going to hire her to work on some of your cases?"

"Hope to."

I put my hand on Milton's confidential file. Ryan still won't reveal who'd hired him to follow me and steal the folder.

"How about if I guess?" I say. "One blink for yes and two for no."

Ryan blinks twice to indicate he doesn't want to play this game.

"I know it has to be either Kingman's son or the writer I met at the Margaret Herrick Library. The guy who ran off when he saw you in West Hollywood. The day you followed me to the Tangent Store."

"Those are your only candidates?"

"How about some shadowy conspiracy figure that wants to suppress Milton's information?"

"Nobody else?"

I stop and think. If the theft is personal, Conrad is the most likely suspect. If the theft is professional, Riley fits the profile. If the theft is a government op, then a conspiracy figure is the answer. What or who else could it be? I'm still not familiar with everything in the folder. I'll have to spend a few days examining every piece of paper and every photograph before I can make an educated guess.

"Do you think the file will be safe here?" I ask. "I mean, will the person who asked you to steal it suspect us?"

"If I were you, I'd find another location for it."

I wonder where to stash the file—and then the perfect spot comes to me.

EIGHTEEN

When I wake up the next morning, it feels late—very, very late. I'm surprised Liam and Lucy haven't jumped on the bed, nudging my cheeks, trying to wake me up. Then I remember that Marelle has once again borrowed the cats to keep Patrick company.

I put my forearm on my forehead and keep my eyes closed, trying to figure out what to do first. I need to take Milton's file to a secure location, somewhere where I can come and go to review the materials.

I also needed to visit a hair salon to have my mangled hair shaped into something presentable—and hope I don't have to get completely shorn into a pixie cut.

But neither of these activities interests me at the moment. What I really want to do is find Shelly Morris, aka Shelby Norris, and ask her some questions about Duke Galveston and Milton Kingman. Joyce told me Shelly hangs out in Beverly Hills— and I figure I'll drive through the area on my way to Pauline Granton's house, where I intend to store Milton's file.

▼

After checking my email, I scan headlines on the *L.A. Times* website, scrolling through the city's never-ending problems with gangs, drugs, and shootings, until I spot a story that makes me feel as if a wrecking ball has hit me in the chest. Nothing I've ever seen or heard has ever shocked me more than this headline: WRITER RILEY TAYLOR KILLED IN CAR CRASH.

Before I can read the article, there's a knock at the door. I recognize the knock.

▼

At the police station, I wait in a conference room, assuming this has something to do with the complaint Conrad Kingman filed against me. While I wait, I pray for the repose of Riley Taylor's soul, using my fingers in the place of rosary beads.

I'm on the third decade of the rosary when the detective glides into the room like a kite with arms and legs.

"Hello, Dakota," he says, "I'm Detective Hernandez."

I nod in greeting. I try to size up the detective—a pleasant-looking man in his mid-forties wearing a white long-sleeved shirt, blue-striped tie, gray dress pants, and shiny black oxfords. I know how to read body language when I'm on the other side of the table conducting the interviews, but not sure how well I can read people when someone else is asking the questions.

"Do you know why you're here?"

"Not really."

"Why do you think you're here?"

"It may have something to do with the writing project I'm doing for Milton Kingman. I was here last night defending myself against false accusations from his son. Officers Flynn and Sanchez handled the matter."

"You were here last night?"

"Yes, but I was able prove that the accusations were false. Milton Kingman even served as a character witness."

"This is quite a coincidence," Detective Hernandez says.

"What is?"

"That you were called here two days in a row for two different matters."

"Why am I here today?"

"Do you know a Riley Taylor?"

"Yes. I saw him yesterday."

"Have you known him long?"

"Since Monday. I met him at the Margaret Herrick Library when I was doing research."

"How many times did you see Mr. Taylor?"

I think for a few seconds before responding.

"Three times," I say. "At the library, then later I visited a wine bar in West Hollywood with him. And yesterday I met him at the Griffith Observatory."

"Were these dates?"

"Not at all," I say. "He was trying to get information from me about Mr. Kingman's project."

"Why was he looking for information?"

I give the detective the outlines of what Riley had told me—about his conspiracy theories related to Duke Galveston, UFOs, aliens, and the government—and that he'd tried to get me to drop Milton Kingman's book project because it would put me in danger.

"Danger, how?" Detective Hernandez asks, setting his elbows on his legs and leaning forward—trying, I assume, to gain my confidence.

"He didn't specify," I answer.

"You were the last person Mr. Taylor contacted on his cell phone."

"I received a text message around four yesterday afternoon."

"Mr. Taylor called you after eleven o'clock last night."

I think for a moment, then remember that I'd left my cell phone in my car while at the police station and while riding back and forth across town in a cab. I explain this to the detective.

"It appears that Mr. Taylor put in a call to you right before his crash."

"What's this all about?" I ask. "If it was a car accident, why are you investigating?"

"We're covering all possibilities," the detective says.

"Well, I've told you everything I know," I say.

"You didn't mention that you and Mr. Taylor had a heated argument outside the Griffith Observatory last night."

I sigh and take deep breaths, trying to calm myself. I can't believe I'm here answering these questions.

"I explained to Mr. Taylor that I'm a ghostwriter and couldn't tell him anything about my assignment. He kept pressuring me to give him confidential materials I'd received from Milton Kingman. When Mr. Taylor wouldn't take no for an answer, I may have raised my voice and told him that I wouldn't give him any information."

122

"How did Taylor know so much about what you were doing?"

"He'd interviewed for the same project. Mr. Kingman considered hiring Taylor and showed him the confidential file. But Mr. Kingman changed his mind and put the project on hold. After a few months, he called me about the job."

"How did he get your contact information?"

"I'm assuming the Internet. I have a website. He probably did a Google search."

"I'll need to talk to Mr. Kingman," Detective Hernandez says.

"Is that really necessary? Mr. Kingman is over eighty years old. This may upset him."

"Why should it?"

"If you lead him to believe Taylor could have been murdered, he may feel threatened, thinking it had something to do with the book he intends to publish. It may cause distress for Mr. Kingman."

"I can't see any way around it, unless you tell me more."

After more prodding, I give a line-by-line account of how I'd become acquainted with Riley Taylor and how our conversations about the Kingman project had evolved.

The detective excuses himself to make a phone call and I use my phone to access the *L.A. Times* and read the article about Taylor's death. The paper has already updated the story to reveal that witnesses to the crash on Olympic near Bundy said that Taylor's Volvo looked as if it had been operated by remote control as it sped up, made a sharp right, and crashed headlong into a palm tree.

◀ NINETEEN ▶

It's four in the afternoon when the patrol car drops me off at my apartment. Detective Hernandez indicated that I can expect subsequent interviews. I dread the thought of the police showing up at Milton's house and consider calling and warning him, but figure this can backfire in a variety of ways—he might think I'd colluded with Riley Taylor, get scared off from completing the book, and ask for the return of his money.

I look around for Ryan's phone number. Where did I put it? After sorting through the papers on my desks and coffee table, I remember that neatnik Ryan had placed his card as a bookmark in my copy of *The Big Sleep*. I text him, saying: "Need to talk to you."

I feel anxious and jumpy, and the last thing I want to do is sit at my computer. I have to get out of the apartment, do something. It's too late to call Pauline about paying a visit, too late to return to the Margaret Herrick Library for more research.

I pour a glass of iced tea and make a sandwich of avocado, red onion, lettuce, and tomato, and eat while thinking about Riley's accident—or was it an accident?

When a person who appears paranoid, spouting secret plots and conspiracy theories, dies under mysterious circumstances, you've got to stop and ask yourself if his suspicions were, in fact, true.

From the Internet, I learn that Taylor was a well-respected investigative journalist in the underground press scene. There are posts on many sites stating that Taylor was working on a "big story"—and had been murdered to keep him quiet.

I do a Google search about the crash, reading various articles until comfortable I have the basic facts related to the incident. I grab my keys and camera and head out of the apartment.

In the parking lot, Joyce is leaning against the trunk of my car, dressed in a—for her—conservative outfit of beige silk blouse, white slacks, and white wedgies, with a black portfolio stashed under her arm. She speaks without even turning to look in my direction, as if she'd expected me to appear at this exact moment.

"I need a ride to Hollywood," Joyce says. "I'm going to test the waters today."

I have no idea what Joyce is talking about, but am not about to ask any questions.

"I'm on my way to work," I tell her.

"It's too late to go to work," Joyce shoots back, then adds: "Isn't it kind of hot for a scarf?"

▼

Five minutes later, I'm driving west on Hollywood Blvd. with Joyce in the passenger seat holding a copy of her Marilyn Monroe drawing. She intends to sell the photocopies for five dollars each outside the Chinese Theater near Hollywood and Highland.

I open the glove box and pull out a five-dollar bill—my emergency gas money.

"Here, I'm your first customer," I say, handing the cash to Joyce.

"I've already sold some around the neighborhood," Joyce replies.

"Oh, you want to test the waters at the Chinese Theater."

"The tourist trade, you know."

"Do you want to try it for a while and have me pick you up in about two hours?"

"What are you going to do in the meantime?"

"I have to shoot some photos on the Westside," I say.

"Okay, yeah," Joyce says. "Pick me up. I hate taking the freaking bus."

▼

Olympic and Bundy is a major intersection with a wide variety of features—mini malls, gas stations, a Cadillac dealership, a gym, a Bed Bath & Beyond, a Staples, a Lamps Plus, a hardware store, and assorted restaurants—but I manage to spot the Riley Taylor shrine a half a block away, thanks to white balloons tied to a palm tree on the southwest corner. I turn left on Bundy, find a parking spot half a block away, and walk back.

As I make my way to the corner, I think about Riley's warnings—and wonder if he was killed as a part of the conspiracy he was trying to expose. Then another thought occurs to me—what if "they" have this shrine under surveillance to see who's paying respects. Am I putting myself in danger by just making a visit? The police have already interviewed me once about my interactions with Riley. Is it smart for me to be here?

Signs are nailed to the palm tree, some with prayers, others with accusations ("this was not an accident," "murdered," and "wiped out" are the major messages). As I read the notes, a feeling comes over me, and I look up to the top of the tree, where the fronds seem to sag in shame. I'm sorry, the tree seems to say, but it wasn't my fault—and, by the way, those nails hurt.

I'll admit I have more than a touch of Attention Deficit Disorder when faced with tragedy—my mind turns to any other topic but the one at hand. I'm more comfortable communing with the tree than thinking about death.

It's hard for me to fathom that Riley is gone, gone, gone, and isn't coming back. When I see the bouquets on the ground, I feel guilty for not bringing flowers.

At the very least, I need to leave a message. I don't carry a hammer and nails, but do have paper, a black marker, and some duct tape. Rather than upset the tree any further, I decide to tape my message to the tail end of another.

I write, "RIP, Riley, you are in my prayers."

▼

I pull up in front of the Chinese Theater—formerly known as Grauman's Chinese Theater—famous since the 1930s for its cement walkway with the footprints, handprints, and signatures of Hollywood royalty.

Double-parking at Hollywood and Highland presents more challenges than trying to do the same at LAX. You cannot linger. You cannot loiter. You cannot lollygag. Your party must hop in your car and off you go.

I look up and down the street, through the web of superhero imitators, Marilyn Monroe lookalikes, and other Hollywood doppelgangers, but don't spot Joyce. The cars behind me blare their horns and a patrolman waves me on. When I don't pull out as fast as the officer commands, he shouts into my open window: "Move it. Now. Or I'm giving you a ticket that'll set you back four hundred bucks."

"Sorry officer," I say.

"She was waiting for me," I hear Joyce tell the officer, as if my old Toyota is a chariot and she's Cinderella.

"Move it!" the cop says.

I turn to Joyce and urge, "Let's go."

"Hold your horses," she says. "You're the one who's been driving around in a comfy car while I've been pounding the pavement in wedgies plying my wares."

Watching Joyce get into the car, shut the door, put her portfolio in the back seat, fasten her seatbelt, and then flip down the visor to examine herself in the mirror, and put on orange lipstick is like watching a slow-motion nature film about the seven-year locust. Good Lord, I think, she really sees herself as a queen and everyone else as her humble servants.

The cop flaps his ticket book at me, saying: "Final warning."

He steps to the rear of the car and studies my license plate. I slip away from the curb just as he's pulling a pen from his pocket. I pray to St. Christopher that a four-hundred-dollar ticket won't appear in the mail. So far, Milton Kingman's project is the most costly job I've ever worked on.

"I'm hungry," Joyce says. "Really hungry. I want Chinese food."

I glance at the clock on the dashboard. It's six o'clock, and we can count on about two more hours of sunlight. I'm not ready to go home and wonder if I can get any more job-related work done tonight. Then it hits me. I can drive to Beverly Hills and we can look for Shelly Morris.

▼

It turns out that Joyce made a hundred dollars by selling twenty photocopies of her Marilyn Monroe drawing.

"I could have sold more, but that's all I brought with me. I stood around smoking and waiting for you to come back."

"Joyce, you're a genius," I say and mean it. The woman has an uncanny aptitude for seeing through people and knowing when something is the right thing to do.

I'm driving west on Wilshire—with the traffic moving at a steady pace, despite rush hour.

"So how many copies do you think you could sell in a day?"

"Depends on how long I want to work."

"Well, taking that into account."

"It's probably better to estimate by the hour. Based on today, I'd say I could sell thirty in an hour. I may even be able to raise the price. I'll have to test out different price points."

It seems Joyce has found her niche. She's a real marketing wiz.

"You seem to know what you're talking about."

"I used to work at Paramount—in accounting and PR. I've always had a knack for numbers and BS."

"Well, if you work for two hours a day and sell sixty copies of the drawing, you'll make over a thousand dollars a week. You have struck gold, Joyce."

"Maybe I'll be able to rent a place. Then again, I don't have any references, so who'll rent to me? God, what you have to show just to rent an apartment these days. Perfect credit score. Two months security deposit, two months rent in advance. I'd probably need a cosigner."

She turns and looks at me, as if studying my profile for a portrait.

"I wish I could help," I say. "But my credit is the worst. I'm barely keeping the wolves from the door."

"How big is your place?"

"One bedroom."

"What do you pay?"

"It's high, that's all I'll say."

"You should move someplace cheaper. Somewhere in the Valley."

"I'm thinking about it."

128

We reach Beverly Hills and drive around for about fifteen minutes, with Joyce in constant motion, looking from side to side, front and back, trying to spot Shelly Morris.

"I'm so freaking hungry," she moans.

"Let's stop and eat," I say.

"Oh," Joyce says and hits herself in the forehead, as if remembering something she should have recalled earlier.

"Oh, what?"

"I know where she probably is."

▼

After a quick stop at a Subway sandwich shop on one of the side streets—with a promise to treat Joyce to Chinese food during the coming week—we make our way toward one of the area's most exclusive locations: The Beverly Hilton Hotel. Good thing neither of us is dressed in shorts and T-shirts.

As I drive into the approaching sundown, I feel a sudden charge—as if I've just awakened after a long and restful sleep. It's as if the light isn't descending into darkness, but is entering my mind and mood. I often feel this way when driving toward the sun at dusk. If gas prices weren't so high, I'd do it more often.

I see the white, L-shaped Beverly Hilton on my left, looming tall and wide—a throwback to the fifties, that beautiful decade between the wars when elegance and good times prevailed.

We park in a lot under the building—and Joyce tells me that we're entitled to two hours of free parking if we buy a drink at the bar and get our ticket validated. I hand Joyce the ticket so she can keep track of it. She seems to enjoy leading the way on this excursion and is reveling in the challenge of finding Shelly Morris.

As we make our way to the lobby, I wonder how much the bar charges for drinks.

▼

The Beverly Hilton lobby bar is a wide-open area set between support pillars and decked out with neo-midcentury sofas, coffee tables, lamps, and upholstered chairs. The lighting is low, the mood is hushed, and the tones are muted. There are plenty of available places to ensconce ourselves for a few hours.

As we stand on the sidelines, acting as if we're looking for someone, I whisper to Joyce, "What makes you think we'll find her here?"

"Oh, look," Joyce says, rushing to the other end of the lobby.

I find her standing before a photograph of Marilyn Monroe, just like the one I'd photocopied for her—the image she'd used to create her drawing.

Joyce seems overwhelmed. Her lips tremble and her eyes fill with tears, as if she's at Lourdes.

"Thank you, Marilyn," Joyce says, touching her fingertips to the glass covering the photograph.

"Please," says an officious-sounding voice behind us.

I turn and see a man in a blue sports jacket with "security" embroidered on his vest pocket.

Joyce's hand drops from the glass and moves to her hair, which she puffs up like a dame in a B movie.

"Sorry, sir," Joyce says, "I was transported for a moment looking at Marilyn's photo. It won't happen again."

The man, a burly guy in his late twenties with military bearing, nods and begins to move away, but Joyce calls after him, "Oh sir."

The man turns, but doesn't say anything. He has more important things to do than tell "hands off" to a Monroe fan. He raises one eyebrow until it forms the semblance of a question mark.

I have no idea what Joyce intends to ask. I'm starting to feel nervous—as if I'm an impostor with no good reason to be in this elegant abode, and I'm about to be exposed as a fraud.

Joyce reaches in her bag and pulls out a photocopy of her Marilyn Monroe drawing. She holds it up to the picture on the wall to show the resemblance. The woman's drafting skills are remarkable—it is an exact copy of the photograph.

"I'm selling these on the Walk of Fame," Joyce tells the security worker. "But, here," she says, holding out the drawing, "I thought you might like to have a copy. This is the only one I have left right now. I saved it in case I ran into someone special. Tell your friends. My email is on the back."

The man takes the drawing from Joyce, looks at it, smiles, then hands it back to her. "Thank you for the offer," he says, "but I can't accept any..." he stops short of saying "bribes" and says, "gifts." He turns and heads out to avert security breaches, quell uprisings, and stamp out rowdies in the microcosm of the world that is the Beverly Hilton Hotel.

After he's about ten feet away, Joyce turns to me and says, "Nice guy."

"What are we doing here, Joyce?" I ask.

But before she can answer, I look up and see someone who looks familiar. It's a pudgy man in his thirties with a buzzcut. I know I've seen this guy recently but can't quite place him.

When he grabs the drawing out of Joyce's hand and glares at me, my memory of him returns in a rush.

He points his finger at me in a "J'accuse" gesture and says, "I knew it!"

It's Wilson from the Margaret Herrick Library—the man who interrogated me about how I intended to use the photocopy he gave me of the copyrighted photograph.

I should have known better than to visit a Beverly Hills bar—since the workers at the library probably unwind after work at nearby watering holes.

Joyce turns to me and says, "What's he talking about?"

While I'm trying to figure out how to respond, I turn to my right and spot Shelly Morris slinking along the wall. Instead of answering Wilson, I rush toward Shelly, who starts to run in three-inch heels. I'm wearing flats, so I soon overtake her. That is, until Wilson overtakes me—grabbing my shoulder and spinning me around.

"I'm talking to you," he says.

I see Shelly's blonde head slip through a door marked "exit."

Wilson tells me that unless Joyce agrees to not sell any copies of the Marilyn Monroe drawing, I'll get permanently banned from the Margaret Herrick Library—and the institution may also hit me with a fine.

Joyce, now standing on my left, promises Wilson she'll destroy all copies of the drawing, a vow that Wilson makes clear he doesn't believe—obvious from his curled lip and buzzcut hairs standing up like porcupine quills.

"If I find out you're selling that image, there will be hell to pay."

I have to fight back a smile. Since Wilson spends most of his time surrounded by movie lore, he's worked famous lines into his conversational repertoire. Hell to Pay? Which John Wayne flick is that from?

"I said I wouldn't, sir," Joyce offers in an apologetic tone I've never heard from her before.

"Make sure you don't," Wilson snaps, then rips the drawing into two pieces, takes the two pieces and rips them into four, then takes the four pieces and rips them into eight.

He slaps the scraps into Joyce's hand, spins around, and heads back to his cohorts from the library—a group I now realize includes Derrick, the handsome researcher. My humiliation is now complete.

Joyce and I exchange looks and take off for the parking lot. When I'm sure we're nowhere within hearing distance of Wilson, I whisper, "Thank you."

"For what?" she says in her normal surly tone.

"Going along with what he said," I tell her. "If I get banned from the library it will affect my ability to earn a living."

"Lighten the eff up, Dakota," she snarls.

I don't have the energy to say anything. God, I can't wait to go to sleep tonight.

When we get to the parking garage, Joyce fires up a ciga-rette. I can't take it any more. I cave in.

"Let me have one," I say, grabbing the pack from her.

Before I get the chance to tap out a smoke, Joyce snatches the package from me.

"You quit. Remember?"

"I stopped," I say, "but I never quit."

Again, I try to grab the pack, but she stuffs it into the back pocket of her slacks.

"Not on my watch," she says.

We've now reached my dusty, mud-splattered car, and I collapse, draping myself across the trunk, allowing the dirt and soot of L.A. to seep into me right down to my bones. I lie here feeling as if I'm inside a grimy seashell, an echoing place that emits a whooooo sound. The odor of tobacco wafts toward me mingled with the scent of night-blooming jasmine, my favorite aromas. I let go of everything. I feel at peace. All is silent for a few moments, until a voice breaks the spell.

"And if he thinks I'm getting rid of those drawings," Joyce says, "he's out of his flipping mind."

◀ TWENTY ▶

The next morning, I check the *L.A. Times* website and find an update about Riley Taylor's car crash. Friends are quoted saying the writer suspected people of tampering with his car, following him, and tapping his phone. My takeaway from the article is that I'm surprised Riley had so many loyal friends. Perhaps I'd misjudged him and should feel grateful that he'd tried to warn me about the Kingman project.

It's just before one in the afternoon when I ring Milton's doorbell. As I wait for him to answer, I take a deep breath and feel a pleasant breeze wash over me. The day is mild, low eighties, with clouds drifting in front of the sun like something in a child's drawing.

The door opens and Milton stands there with a cup in his hand. Rather than greet me or voice surprise that I've stopped by, he says, "Care for some coffee, Dakota?"

Well, at least he remembers my name.

We sit outdoors at a table shaded by an umbrella, with a glass carafe of coffee beside us, drinking from Mikasa china cups in a Blue Point pattern. The mood is serene—far, far away from the hot rush of Hollywood. I appreciate spending even half an hour learning how the other half lives.

I hate to break the spell, but need to get to the point sooner or later, so take a deep breath and pull the *L.A. Times* from my bag.

I point to Riley Taylor's photo on the front page and ask, "Do you recognize this man?"

Milton leans over and takes a quick look, then shakes his head. "No," he says.

"Can I ask a favor?" I say.

"Anything," he offers, stretching his arms wide.

"Would you put on your glasses and take a closer look?"

The right corner of Milton's mouth rises—a movement that I've come to realize indicates mild amusement.

"They're on my nightstand."

"Do you want me to get them?"

"Well, you move a whole lot faster than I do," he replies.

After Milton explains how to find his bedroom, I head into the house. When stepping across the threshold, I realize it's probably not a good idea to enter this room. What if Milton's son barges in unannounced and finds me here? Lord, the perils of working for elderly clients with suspicious children. It makes me downright paranoid.

On the nightstand, I find Milton's glasses next to a framed portrait of a beautiful blonde in her twenties. I figure this must be Milton's deceased wife, Geraldine—a face I've seen before. I guess the only time Milton puts on his glasses is before bed when he gazes at Geraldine's photograph.

I hesitate, then pick up the photo and head back outside.

When I hand Milton his glasses, he puts them on and sees that I've set the framed photograph on the table.

"Who is this?" I ask, pointing to the picture.

"Why, Geraldine, of course," he says. "Only woman I've ever loved. And it's the only photo I have of her."

"Why is that?"

"Conrad took all of them."

"I know someone who has more," I tell him.

▼

Thirty minutes later, Milton is in the passenger seat of my car and we're driving north on Sepulveda toward Pauline Granton's place in Bel Air.

Milton has a big smile on his face—the first time I've seen him with both corners of his mouth turned up at the same time.

"You look happy," I say.

"I love going for rides."

"That makes two of us, especially when I'm not driving."

I fumble in the back seat until I find the *L.A. Times*, then set it on Milton's lap. I reach into my bag, pull out Milton's eyeglasses, and place them on top of the newspaper.

"Would you take a look at this photo," I say, pointing to Riley Taylor's picture on the front page.

Milton puts on his glasses and moves the paper closer to his face.

"Should I know him?" he asks.

"I met this man a few days ago when I was doing research at the Margaret Herrick Library. He claimed to know you."

"I've met thousands of people over the years."

Milton starts to read the article, then looks over at me.

"So this fellow died in a car crash."

"Yes."

"What are you getting at, Dakota?"

"The man in the photo, Riley Taylor, said he'd met with you about ghostwriting your book."

"I interviewed a few people before I picked you. You should feel flattered."

"Depends on why you picked me."

"I always follow my instincts," he said. "Of all the people I met with, I thought I could work best with you."

"Thanks," I say, but need to stay on the subject. "Riley told me that you showed him the research materials, the file you gave me."

"I might have."

"Well, he believed the material could prove one of his conspiracy theories. He said the project would put me in danger and advised me to quit."

"I told you the project was dangerous," Milton said. "Everybody who knows about this has died under mysterious circumstances. I'm so old now that it doesn't matter anymore."

"And you're not worried about me?"

"You're supposed to be a ghostwriter."

"Milton, your son knows I'm working on your book. The police know I'm working on your book. Riley Taylor figured out I was working on your book. Pauline Granton knows I'm working on your book. So if certain people don't want this story to get out, I'm already in trouble."

"Occupational hazard," Milton says.

"Milton, I write puff pieces, light, fluffy fare. 'My Life in the Golden Age of Hollywood,' that sort of thing. I'm not an investigative journalist prepared to take on the forces of darkness."

"I'm sorry that Conrad and the police found out," Milton says. "I should have paid you in cash, then Conrad wouldn't have been able to snoop into my bank account."

He takes off his glasses and stuffs them back in the case, which he tosses onto the dashboard. As I make a right onto Skirball Drive, Milton turns to stare at me.

"Sorry, Dakota," Milton says, "but you're the one who let this Taylor fellow and Pauline know what you were doing. I guess we're both to blame."

▼

I take a deep breath before I put my hand on the lion door-knocker and announce my arrival at Pauline Granton's house. There are so many things I need to do here today, but I didn't call in advance to announce my intentions. I figure Pauline will still feel in my debt because her husband attacked me during my last visit.

But before I can knock, the door flings open and Pauline greets me with open arms.

"Dakota!" she says. "So happy to see you."

She looks at my green tiger-striped scarf and shakes her head.

"You should have let me give you a hat."

"Thanks," I say, "but I plan to get a haircut later today."

"Well, come on in," she tells me, then offers her megawatt smile.

I look over to my car, where Milton is waiting. Pauline follows my gaze and squints her eyes, trying to make out who's in the car.

"Is that your grandfather?" she asks.

I take a long inhale, as if taking a drag on a cigarette, and say, "Pauline. It's Milton Kingman. We were out for a ride, and I thought I'd take a chance and drop by."

"Milton Kingman!" Pauline says, running toward the car.

Milton sees her rushing toward him and gets out of the Toyota. He moves closer to her, and they meet under a giant ficus tree. They hold out their arms to each other and embrace.

"Beautiful as ever," Milton says as he looks up into Pauline's face.

Pauline is about 5'5" and Milton is no more than 5'2"—and I sense for the first time that he's self-conscious about his height.

"Handsome as ever," Pauline responds.

"Except I've shrunk four inches," he says.

"Could have fooled me," she tells him.

As the person tasked with writing Milton Kingman's life story, it's great to know that a friend from the past holds him in such high regard. Call me crazy, but I want to love and admire everyone I write about.

"Well come on in and visit for a while," Pauline says, putting her arm around Milton's shoulder and leading him toward her house.

As we enter, I have to stop myself from telling Milton keep his hat on.

◀ TWENTY-ONE ▶

During the next few hours, Milton exudes happiness. I perceive all kinds of new things about him—especially that he thrives in good company and is a lively and thoughtful companion.

Pauline, too, seems bubbling over with joy. I realize how lonely she must be staying home most of the time, overwhelmed with worry about her husband.

She and Milton talk nonstop from the time we arrive, through lunch—which Pauline orders from a nearby Chinese restaurant—and during coffee and dessert. They catch up on a half century of personal history, but for the most part talk about their time working with Duke Galveston—and it feels as if they've been transported back to the 1950s in a time machine.

Pauline explains Albert's condition and tells Milton she thinks it best if her husband stays in the family room with his nurse during the visit. She wants Milton to remember Albert the way he was.

"I'd like to at least shake his hand and say hello," Milton tells her.

"Right before you leave would be a good time."

When Pauline offers more coffee and Milton accepts, I know he's not yet ready to leave. I follow Pauline into the kitchen to get a private word with her.

I spill out my request—that I want to store some confidential material in her safe and come back another time to review the file along with her memorabilia.

"Of course, dear," she tells me. I wonder whether to mention Riley Taylor's warnings about the material, but decide it would be too complicated to explain.

"Thank you, Pauline."

She puts her hand on my shoulder and says, "Thank you, Dakota, for bringing Milton to see me. This is the most fun I've had in years."

"I'm sure he feels the same way."

When we return to the living room, Milton is gone. We look in the dining room and the backyard, but he isn't there. Soon, we hear loud voices coming from the other end of the house. Pauline and I rush toward the family room.

After we enter, Pauline stands in the doorway taking in the scene. Milton is sitting next to Albert on the red plaid sofa and the two men seem to be engaged in conversation. Albert's nurse sits in a chair by the window, eyes wide and face frozen—as if she's stunned.

I try to make myself invisible by standing behind a floor lamp and remaining still. When I glance at Pauline, she has tears rolling down her face. My guess is that Albert hasn't been this coherent in years. Milton's presence has jumpstarted Pauline's husband back to an awareness of who he is, where he is, and what's happened in his life. I wonder how long this miracle will last. Maybe Milton will have to move in.

Now that the shock of Albert's lucidity has worn off a bit, both Pauline and I move closer to the sofa to catch every word of the men's conversation.

"Don't mention you-know-who," Pauline whispers to Milton, referring to Duke Galveston, the name that sent Albert into a tirade during my previous visit.

Milton nods, but Albert turns to Pauline and says, "Milton can mention anyone he likes, including a certain horse's ass named Duke Galveston."

"I thought you were such good friends," Milton says.

"At one time," Albert replies.

"What happened?

"I don't think this is a good topic for discussion," Pauline says, then puts her hand on Albert's shoulder. She bends down, plants a kiss on her husband's forehead, then looks in his eyes and says, "How are you, honey?"

"Milton is here," he tells Pauline.

"Yes, it's wonderful to see him after all these years."

I move to get a better view of Albert's expression, and when I do he notices me for the first time.

"Who's that woman in the scarf?" Albert says, pointing to me.

Before I can respond, Milton says, "That's Dakota Donovan, my assistant."

"What are you working on these days, Milt?" Albert says.

"Right now, a book. My life story."

Albert's mouth opens wide, as if he's just remembered something.

"How's Geri?" Albert asks.

Milton lets the air out of his lungs in a gush, as if something is pressing on his chest. He doesn't respond for at least thirty seconds. Finally, he manages to say, "Geraldine passed away two years ago. We were married for fifty-three years."

Albert starts to say something, but before he can speak, Milton turns to Pauline and says, "Dakota tells me you have some photographs of my wife."

"Oh, yes," Pauline responds. "I'll go and get them."

"Are they in the same place?" I ask. When she nods, I say, "Let me do it."

Five minutes later, when I'm still collecting photographs of Geraldine, Pauline steps into the dining room. She collapses in a chair and puts her hands over her face as if trying to stop the deluge that follows. Her sobbing is silent, and I know she's trying to hide her tears from the two men in the other room.

A few minutes later, Pauline takes in short, hiccupy breaths and says, "After all this time, I can't believe it."

I put my hand on Pauline's shoulder.

"It's been years since Albert could carry on a conversation," she tells me.

"Seeing someone from the past must have shocked his brain in some way," I offer.

"I'm afraid to hope this will last," she says.

"Maybe we should try to find some of Albert's other old friends," I say, then mention that I'd spotted Shelly Morris at the Beverly Hilton the previous evening.

"Oh, no," Pauline says, "not Shelly Morris. She's what broke up Duke and Albert's friendship."

"How?" I ask.

"Duke had girls, many of them still teenagers, set up in houses all over L.A.," she says. "They were kept under lock and key. Shelly was Duke's particular favorite, but she was a wild one. She liked to sneak out and go drinking and dancing. When Duke found out that Albert knew what Shelly was up to but didn't tell him, that was the end. The only good thing that came of it was that Duke had Shelly move in with him so he could keep an eye on her. He almost married her, but at least he left her the house."

"Well, she's homeless now," I say.

"So very sad," Pauline responds. She sighs, then stands up. "Well, we'd better get back."

I put the stack of photos in a manila folder and follow Pauline to the family room.

When we get there, Albert and Milton are both laughing over some mutual recollection. Albert's nurse meets us at the doorway.

"Mrs. Simms, do you mind if I step out for a bit?" she asks.

"Of course, Sarah, take the rest of the day off."

Sarah's face lights up as if she's won a two-week vacation in Hawaii. I guess an afternoon away from major responsibility can seem that way.

I take a seat next to Milton and hand him the folder. Before opening it, he pats his pockets.

"Here," I say, handing him his glasses.

He puts them on with great care, as if about to perform a delicate operation.

"Ah," he says when he picks up the first picture, showing Geraldine in a bathing suit at the beach.

He takes his time going from one photo to another. I turn to Albert, who's watching Milton as if he can read the other man's soul.

"I'm sorry about Geri," Albert says.

"Thank you, Albert," Milton responds.

Pauline stands behind the sofa with her hands on Albert's shoulders, watching Milton as he stares at the photos of Geraldine.

"Where did you get all of these?" Milton asks.

"I've been collecting for years," Pauline says.

"So you purchased these photos?" Milton asks.

"Most of them, yes," Pauline answers.

"Where?"

"Different places."

"eBay?"

"Some of them, yes."

Milton turns and looks at me. I'm not sure what he intends to say or do. But before he can respond to Pauline, Albert starts pounding on his knees with his fists.

"I'm sorry about Geri. I'm sorry about Geri. I'm sorry about Geri," he yells.

Pauline pats his shoulder and says, "Yes, dear, we know you are."

"No! No!" Albert cries. "Not that she's dead, but I'm sorry about that, too."

"Calm down, dear," Pauline leans down and whispers in Albert's ear.

"I'm sorry I didn't help her. I'm sorry," he says, covering his face with his hands. "I'm so ashamed."

"What's he talking about?" Milton asks Pauline, but the woman just shrugs and shakes her head.

"I'm sorry, Geri. I'm sorry, Geri . . ."

▼

Five minutes later, Milton and I are in my car headed back to Brentwood. He's silent and withdrawn, the opposite of his elated mood when we arrived at Pauline Granton's place. I don't know whether it's best to say something or say nothing. In these cases, I usually err on the side of something.

"Do you know what Albert was talking about?" I ask.

Milton doesn't respond for a full minute, then says, "Please, Dakota, just take me home."

▼

After I drop off Milton and get him settled in his house, I sit in my car checking my text messages. Still no answer from Ryan, so I sent him another message: "Need to see you. Urgent."

I take Sepulveda to Olympic and head east in the afternoon rush. I zone out, listening to KUSC-FM—Barber's "Adagio for Strings" putting me in a melancholy mood. After a few minutes, I realize I'm near the site of Riley Taylor's accident, make a right at Bundy, and pull into a spot near the corner.

Staring out the back window, I see a tree filled with multi-colored balloons. If I didn't know its purpose, I'd think the display had something to do with a Disney flick. Votive candles and bouquets of flowers encircle the tree, plus there's something new—small American flags.

When I spot messages taped and nailed to the tree, I want to get out and read each one, but already have the basic idea from the newspaper stories—people think Riley Taylor's accident was no accident.

As the cellos mourn from the radio, I start to sob from somewhere deep, deep within. I feel guilty about how I treated Riley Taylor and regret that I didn't appreciate what he wanted to do for me. Instead, I suspected him of trying to steal my story. Writers are such untrusting creatures. Anyway, I am.

I allow myself to cry for a while, my hands gripping the steering wheel as I let the sadness overwhelm me.

I close my eyes and fall into a dark place—not asleep, not awake, a deep well with no bottom. It seems bad and good at the same time—sorrowful yet purging. I feel that the well is filling with water, and I'm floating up, up, up toward the top, toward the light.

When I open my eyes, I don't know how much time has passed. I sigh, take a deep breath, check my rearview mirror, and pull into the street. When I do, a dark car pulls out behind mine.

As I make a couple of left turns and then a right to get back onto Olympic, it's clear that the car behind me is on my tail—and not even trying to hide its pursuit.

◀ TWENTY-TWO ▶

I can think of only two possibilities. The person behind me is either Ryan—still following me for a client—or it's Conrad, who was waiting outside his father's house when I dropped off Milton.

I feel feverish, my head throbs, and my stomach aches. Oh, God, how I wish an angel driver would appear to chauffeur me home.

At Westwood Boulevard, I notice a gas station on my right and make a sharp turn into it. I pull up next to a pump and check my rearview mirror. When I don't spot anyone behind me, I look to the street and see that the black car is at the curb.

I make my way into the gas station mini-mart and purchase a bottle of Lipton's iced tea, a package of Lorna Doone cookies, and a bottle of Excedrin. After paying, I stand at the counter and swallow two Excedrin with the tea, then open the cookies and take small bites of one, trying to calm my stomach.

As I stand there, a strange idea enters my head. It's so outrageous and outlandish that I wonder where it came from or what made me think of it. There's only one way to find out.

I march back to my car, pull out of the station, and park behind the black SUV that's been following me. I hop out and rush toward the passenger side door. I yank on the door, and it opens. When I look inside, I see my hunch was correct.

The person driving the car is Riley Taylor.

I recognize the driver, even though his head is shaved and he's dressed like a surfer in a sleeveless T-shirt and baggy shorts.

"Get in," he says in a rough whisper.

I hesitate for a split second, and in that minuscule amount of time consider the pros and cons of each alternative. It's a scary prospect getting into the vehicle of someone who's supposed to be dead. And, who knows, he might be a worse driver than I am. But how can I pass up the chance to find out what this is all about?

I slide into the SUV, put on my seatbelt, and lean back as Riley glides into traffic. What time is it? The light is starting to fade. It must be after seven.

Neither of us speaks. I catch a glimpse of myself in the visor mirror and see that I have mascara marks down my cheeks, as if I'm Pagliacci. I wonder what the people at the gas station thought when they saw me.

Riley grabs a tissue from the center console and hands it to me. I daub at my cheeks as he drives, but the black lines won't come off. I reach in my bag and pull out a tube of hand cream, rubbing some on my face and then wiping away my black tears.

"Where are we headed?" I ask.

Riley laughs and says, "You're succinct. I'll give you that."

"I figure you'll let me know what's going on when you're ready," I say.

"Good," he says. "Because I planned to tell you 'no questions.'"

"None?"

"Okay, one."

"Who was in the car?"

"Next question," he says, then turns to me. "And now I have one for you."

"Shoot," I say.

"Do you still have my sunglasses?"

I reach into the pocket of my bag and take them out.

"Here you go," I say as I hand him the Ray Bans.

"Good thing they weren't in my car when it crashed," he says.

"Good thing," I repeat.

"Another migraine?" Riley says a few minutes later, as we head west on Wilshire.

"Why do you ask?"

"I saw you taking Excedrin at the gas station," he says. "You can spot that green bottle from fifty feet away."

"Just a headache. Not a migraine."

"I didn't know you cared," he says, and I know he's referring to my recent crying jag.

"I felt guilty. I'm not sure that's the same as caring," I say.

"Guilty that you didn't listen to me?" he offers.

"Something like that."

"So what do you think happened?" he asks.

I know he's testing me to see if I've figured out how he arose from the dead. I take a deep breath, close my eyes, think for a minute, and then turn to look at him. It's obvious that he's adopted a new identity.

"So what are you calling yourself these days?" I ask.

"Raymond," he tells me.

"Last name?" I ask, then add, "And don't say Chandler."

"Shipley," he says. "Raymond Shipley."

"Can I call you Ray?"

"I prefer Raymond."

"All right, Raymond," I say. "I want to give you the benefit of the doubt. I want to believe you had nothing to do with the crash or setting up the person who died in it."

"Go on," he says.

"Where are we going?" I ask.

"We need to talk. I need to eat. It's someplace secluded. I'll get you back to your car by ten."

I open my bottle of Lipton's iced tea and take a long drink. Then I let my eyes go into soft focus, inviting the twilight to move through me. I relax into my seat and enjoy the ride. When I open my window, I can smell the ocean. I take in a long, long breath and feel as if I'm floating like a balloon toward the sea.

At Ocean Avenue in Santa Monica, Riley turns right. I see the Santa Monica Pier in the distance, and soon we're on Pacific Coast Highway headed north.

"So finish what you were saying," Riley tells me.

That's the last thing I want to do. I'm content to not say another word and let somebody else do the driving.

"Well . . ."

I sigh. I try to make my comment short and to the point.

"What about the dental records?"

"I don't have dental records," he says. "Under my own name, anyway."

"What about the person who died in the crash?"

"Just a drifter."

"With no crowns or fillings?"

"Lucky coincidence," he says.

"So how did the drifter happen to drive your Volvo?"

"Pure chance," he says. "I was walking down Hollywood Blvd. and a guy came up to me, a panhandler. The first thing I noticed was how much he looked like me. Around the same age, the same height, same coloring."

Riley pulls off the road at a spot where a billboard announces "Malibu Fish Shack." After parking the car, he turns to me.

"I asked him if he wanted to make a hundred bucks," he says.

He waits for a few seconds, as if giving me time to process his words.

"And you asked him to drive your car somewhere while you followed in another vehicle," I say.

"Right," Riley says, then adds, "I saw the accident."

"And you don't feel guilty about what happened?"

"I'm not the one who tampered with the car. I'm not the one who tried to kill me," he says.

"Yes, but you're the one who asked an innocent bystander to drive the car."

"He had a choice."

"But not all the information."

"What's done is done," he says. "I can't undo it."

"But you were prepared, just in case," I say. "Weren't you?"

"I had a Plan B," he says, "which I'm now carrying out."

"You had a new identity established before the accident," I say.

"As I said, I had a backup."

"So what are you going to do now?"

"You can learn a lot when people think you're dead," he says.

Before I have a chance to ask anything else, Riley says, "If you're hungry, you'll have to save your questions. This place closes at eight."

▼

It's 7:55 when we take our heaping trays onto the patio. This is the best seafood place I've seen on the West Coast, and I can't wait to dig into my feast—the Seafood Combination (fish, shrimp, scallops, squid & fries). Riley ordered the same, plus a loaf of fresh baked bread. From his trunk, he removes a cooler with four bottles of Heineken.

As we take our seats under the patio umbrellas—the last straggling customers on this weekday in August—the sun is just about to say adios. I watch it sink below the horizon, like an eye closing—just that fast. The Pacific has no one to watch over it until tomorrow morning. The water gives off melancholy feeling, as if sad that the sun has abandoned it once again.

Riley appears ravenous, digging into his food as if he hasn't eaten for days. I decide not to interrupt his feeding time with any questions and set about to devour the fish and chips—my second favorite meal in the world, after grilled cheese sandwiches. While I mainly eat a vegetarian diet, I'm always ready to make an exception for fried fish.

In my head, Fred Astaire starts to sing, "Heaven, I'm in heaven"—the meal is that amazing. My opinion of Riley has gone up about fifty notches—I mean, how can you not like someone who introduces you to such a great spot?

After finishing half my meal and drinking a Heineken, I lean back, sigh, and look across the road toward the ocean. It's a postcard-perfect evening, the moonless sky and sea merging into one mysterious slate-blue mass.

"Are you going to finish that?" Riley asks, pointing to my food. It's the first time he's spoken since we'd started to eat.

"Taking a break for a minute," I say.

I really want to save the rest of the food for later. I'm one of those awful people who loves to eat before going to bed—what the doctors and health nuts say never to do.

"Would you like some?" I ask.

In the flickering light from the Tiki candle, I see Riley's eyes sparkle.

"If you don't want any more," he says.

After a few moments, I say, "Go ahead."

I know I'll have a lingering unsatisfied feeling because I didn't finish the food—a meal I was relishing. I'll have to come back here soon—if I can get someone to drive me.

I push my paper plate toward Riley, and he seems to bow his head toward me in gratitude.

As he eats, I try to remember how many days since his supposed death. Two? Three? Has he not eaten the whole time? Or does he always eat this much?

"When you said secluded, you weren't exaggerating," I say.

Riley takes a long swallow of beer, sits up straight, pulls air into his lungs, and says, "Great spot. You can see all the cars in the lot and notice whenever someone pulls in."

Just then, my cell phone beeps with a text message. Riley recoils as if it's the executioner calling to say his time is up. I push the phone toward him. Does he suspect that it's an accomplice calling to find out my location for the real kill?

"Here," I say. "Read it to me."

He picks up the phone and reads, "What do you need to see me about? R."

Riley pushes the phone back to me.

"Do you need to answer it?"

"If you're here, I can ask you the question."

"Which is . . .?"

"Did you hire someone to follow me?"

With both hands, he pushes himself about a foot from the table and shakes his head.

"It wasn't me."

150

"You wouldn't lie, would you? Not after I gave you the rest of my fish."

He shakes his head and asks, "Any other suspects?"

I give him the short version of what happened with Milton's son and my trip to the Hollywood police station.

"Outrageous," he says. "I'd like to kick Conrad's ass."

"Thanks, but I handled it. He won't bother me anymore."

"Then who's having you followed?"

"You didn't even question it. How do you know I was followed?"

"I don't think you'd imagine something like that."

"So do you plan on remaining Raymond Shipley or is this just a temporary incarnation?"

"I have a number of options," he says, opening another beer. "If I figure out who's trying to wipe me out, I can come out of hiding, explain what happened, and become Riley Taylor once again."

"So is that why you were at the crash site? Looking for who showed up?"

"Basically."

"Pardon my asking. But what kind of freelance writer can afford to go on the lam?"

"Not every writer is as broke as you are, Dakota."

"You must play the stock market."

"I used to."

"You must be good at it."

"I used to be."

He hands me another beer, but I shake my head.

"Heineken's and Excedrin are not the most healthy combination."

He drains his second beer, starts to open a third one, but instead tosses the bottle back in the cooler.

I smell the sand and the sea and hear the seagulls calling overhead. In the darkness, I stare at the outline of Riley's shaved head and get the sense that I'm looking at someone just born.

As if reading my thoughts, he says, "You're the only person who knows."

I can't decide whether to feel flattered or frightened, and wonder why he picked me to confide in.

"I wasn't planning on telling anyone," he adds.

"Why did you change your mind?"

"When I saw you crying at the crash site, it was like all my defenses broke down. It seemed wrong to let you go on thinking I was dead."

"So where are you living?" I ask.

"Why don't you let me show you?" he says.

◀ TWENTY-THREE ▶

When we get into the car, Riley holds up a blue bandana and says, "I hate to ask you to do this."

I have no idea what's coming. Is he going to ask me to dust the dashboard? Before I can think of any other uses for a bandana, he says, "I'll take you where I'm living, but I can't let you know where it is."

I get the point. In case anyone asks, I can say that I don't know—and not give myself away with a guilty look.

"You want to blindfold me?"

"Like I said, I hate to ask," he tells me.

"Don't you think it'll look strange if you're driving around with someone wearing a blindfold?"

"That's what the Ray Bans are for."

So five minutes later, we're driving down some road somewhere. The blue bandana is tied around my eyes, and I'm wearing Riley's sunglasses over the blindfold.

I try to get a sense of which direction we're headed, but since the windows are closed, I can't hear much or feel the night air. This is definitely one of the stranger experiences of my life.

Without my sense of sight, I feel dizzy and disoriented. I keep wondering how long the drive will take. But then I realize that even if Riley lives five minutes from the seafood restaurant, he'll drive around to make it seem as if his place is farther away.

I decide to let go, lean back, and just float along. I hear Riley press a button on the dashboard, and a few moments later a song begins to play—Louis Armstrong singing "Moon River," an all-time favorite. There is something surreal and sublime about listening to this particular song while blindfolded and traveling to who-knows-where.

"Was that a commentary?" I ask after the song ends.

"How so?"

"'Two drifters, off to see the world . . .'"

"No hidden meanings," he says. "I just like the song. How about you?"

"You haven't been spying on my Spotify selections, have you?"

When he doesn't respond, I add, "Well . . ."

"Oh, sorry," he tells me. "I shook my head to say no."

"And you've already forgotten I'm blindfolded."

"The sunglasses are a good disguise."

"I hope you've got some food at your place," I say.

"We just ate."

"You ate," I say. "I was just getting started."

▼

When the car comes to a stop, I start to remove the Ray-Bans and blindfold, but Riley reaches out and grabs my left hand, saying, "Wait until we get inside. Believe me, it's for your own good."

I wait while he walks around to the passenger side, opens the door, and helps me out. He puts my left hand in the crook of his right arm and leads me down a path. I hear a gate creak open and then close a few moments later. Riley ushers me down another path, then veers toward the left, and up a short flight of stairs. I hear him open the door with a key. He leads me inside, then closes the door.

"Can I unblindfold myself?" I ask.

Riley doesn't respond. Instead, he walks up to me, takes off the Ray-Bans, sets them aside, then puts both hands behind my head and unties the bandana, which he removes with a flourish—like a magician uncovering a rabbit in a hat.

I look up at him and he looks down at me, and we definitely share a moment. It's the kind of moment in a detective movie when the private eye kisses the mysterious stranger. And that might have happened if my cell phone hadn't started to ring. Riley grabs the phone from my bag, turns it over, and removes the battery.

"I should have done that earlier," he says.

He's talking about the phone's GPS system—worried that someone may track me here and find him.

He stuffs the phone and battery back into my bag. "Sorry I had to do that," he says.

"You're sorry about a lot of things tonight," I tell him.

"I'm sorry you never let me see the Milton Kingman file."

"Oh, right," I say, "before you died you kept asking me to show it to you."

"Now maybe you'll believe I have a reason to see it."

For the first time, I take a look at the surroundings. I do a full three-sixty and view the whole place from the same spot. I don't know if it's a small apartment or a small house—I'm thinking the latter, considering how we entered. It feels like something from an old-school bungalow court—dining area, living room, bedroom, and railroad kitchen. The furniture is Seventies funky, definitely thrift store finds, not, I imagine, Riley's taste at all.

I can tell that Riley is seeing the place through my eyes. He smiles.

"Not what you expected," he says. "I picture you as a mid-century modern aficionado."

I turn and give him my Dirty Harry squint. "And you're not snooping on me?"

"Just making some lucky guesses that we have the same taste in music and furniture."

I walk into the kitchen and look in the refrigerator—a dozen eggs, a loaf of whole wheat bread, sliced cheddar, and a pound of butter. I figure we have the same taste in food as well, but stop short of asking him to make me a grilled cheese sandwich. I'm starting to feel anxious about the situation, too nervous to eat.

When I spot a box of Lipton tea bags on top of the refrigerator, it seems as if I've found the elixir of life. Nothing would suit me better at this moment than a cup of tea. I pour water from a plastic jug into a teakettle and turn on the electric burner. I find a couple of cups in the dish drainer.

While I busy myself with the tea, Riley excuses himself and heads toward what I assume is the bathroom. During his absence, I make a quick tour of the living room to see what I can see. The only thing I find is a copy of *The Big Sleep*, the same edition I have at home. It's getting harder and harder to believe that all of these common interests are coincidences.

"Great book," I hear Riley say when he returns to the room.

"As you know," I tell him, "it's one of my favorites."

"How would I know?"

"That's what I'd like to know."

Before he can respond, the teakettle starts to whistle.

A few minutes later, we're sitting on the orange tweed sofa sipping tea and trying to act as if the situation isn't awkward. In cases like this, I do what I always do: ask questions of all types—inane, arcane, mundane—anything to keep the conversation rolling.

After I ask how he came to live in this spot, Riley informs me that he found a sublet on Craigslist and had no problem renting the place for three months without offering any references. The people were in a hurry to leave—they were New-Agers who at the last minute had decided to tour alien crop circle sites in the U.K.—and since he had the rent money plus a two-month security deposit, they were happy to hand him the keys and take off.

"It doesn't get much more anonymous than this," he says.

"So who do you think is trying to kill you?" I ask.

"I have a list of suspects," he tells me. "For your own good, it's best that you don't know."

I tell him that the person tailing me stole the Milton Kingman file, but then returned it—and I stashed it in a secure location.

"Whoa," he says, "back up."

I grab my bag and root around for my e-cigarette. After firing it up, I explain about Ryan and how the detective took pity on me and returned the file.

"Who hired him?"

"I thought it was you."

"Not me," he says, shaking his head.

"I know almost nothing about you, Riley."

"I love fried fish, Louis Armstrong, Raymond Chandler, grilled cheese sandwiches, and Danish Modern furniture," he says. "How's that for a start?"

"So you're not going to tell me about yourself, your project, or who's trying to kill you," I say.

"Let's talk about you," he tells me.

"Me? I'm just a middle-aged divorcee with grown kids trying to make a living as a writer in some way, shape, or form."

"You're not middle-aged," he says.

"I'm in my forties."

"That's not middle aged."

I take a sip of now-lukewarm tea and a drag on my e-cigarette. I know I'm just a lightweight writer and no match for an investigative journalist like Riley Taylor, but I think I've figured out this case. Whether or not it solves Riley's case is another matter.

"I paid a couple of visits to an actress who made films for Duke Galveston," I say.

"Which one?"

"Let's just leave out her name for now," I say.

"Go on," he says, moving closer.

"She told me that Duke was a practical joker with a cruel streak," I say, then stop for a moment to recall Pauline Granton's words. All the pieces are snapping together. I see the full picture.

"So Duke was a practical joker. So what?" Riley says.

"So, I believe that all of those alien photos were an elaborate hoax—something Duke staged to make Milton believe they were visited by aliens. Milton put so much trust in Duke that he never doubted him for a second. He's lived for decades with this deep, dark secret that wasn't a secret at all. It was a joke—something staged with props, costumes, and actors from Duke's sci-fi flicks."

Riley leans back and stares at the ceiling, as if trying to process what I've just told him.

"So those photos," I say, "the photos you've been trying so hard to get your hands on, are in effect nothing more than movie stills."

"If that's true, you've just put yourself out of a job," Riley says.

I get his point. Milton hired me to write the story about his alien visitations. I'll have to sell him on a different book. But how do I break the news that his good friend Duke Galveston duped him and kept on duping him for years?

"I'll take the chance," I tell him.

As soon as I say this, Riley's head falls back as if he's been shot. I'm stunned, wondering what happened—concerned that he might have had a stroke from all the stress he's been under. When he lets out a loud snore, I realize he's passed out from exhaustion. He's probably been up for days, and this is the first time he's let himself relax, even a little.

Now what? The good part is that Marelle is taking care of Liam and Lucy, so I don't have to worry about the cats. I'm tempted to tiptoe to the front door, make my exit, figure out where I am, and head for home—just stick the battery back in my phone and call for an Uber. But I promised not to do that—at least I gave Riley an implied promise. I pad over to the window in my stocking feet, lift the slats in the mini blinds and look outside. I was right. It is a bungalow court—what looks like a half dozen tiny houses surrounding a courtyard of grass and flowers.

The lyrics from "L.A. Woman" come back to me: " . . . with a little girl in a Hollywood bungalow. Are you a lucky little lady in the city of light or just another lost angel?"

A snore from the sofa breaks the spell. I step into the bedroom and grab a light blanket, then go back to the living room and cover Riley. I'm not tired at all. The tea was probably a bad idea so late at night.

I sit in the chair opposite the sofa, put my feet on an ottoman, and crack open *The Big Sleep*, picking up just where I left off.

◀ TWENTY-FOUR ▶

I open my eyes and look around. I have no idea where I am and wonder whether I'm awake or asleep. I hear some kind of chanting coming from outside, but can't understand what the people are saying. Is this a dream? I feel as if my heart is in the middle of my throat.

I turn to the window and see light coming through the closed blinds. It's starting to come back to me. I'm in the bungalow Riley rented from the New-Agers who are in England touring crop circle sites. But where's Riley?

When I stand up, a book falls to the floor—*The Big Sleep*. I fell asleep reading it.

The chanting sounds like Ba-Da-Ba-Da-Ba-Da-Bom over and over—sometimes high-pitched and sometimes at a lower level. It's a blend of men's and women's voices.

I check the bedroom, the bathroom, and the kitchen, but Riley is G-O-N-E. I know he doesn't want me to leave, because if I walk out the door, I'll figure out where I am.

When I start to make myself a cup of tea, I spot a note attached to the refrigerator with a flying saucer magnet. It's short and to the point: D, Don't leave. Be right back. R.

I'd like nothing better than to take a shower, or, better yet, a bath, but have visions of Janet Leigh getting slaughtered in *Psycho*. I find a clean washcloth and towel in a dresser drawer and take a sponge bath and rub some toothpaste around in my mouth with my finger.

When I look in the mirror to wash my face, I realize that my scarf is missing. I've been wearing it for so many days in a row that it's become second nature, the way you don't notice your glasses after wearing them for a while. I figure it must have come off when I was sleeping in the chair.

Just as I enter the living room, Riley walks in the front door. When he opens it, I get the full effect of the nerve-wracking chanting. Lord, get me out of here. If there's one thing that drives me nuts it's intrusive noises. I just can't block them out.

When he sees me, Riley tilts his head to one side, as if looking at a painting that he can't figure out. Well, now he's seen my Cubist haircut. I don't have to try to hide it anymore.

"I'd ask what happened to you," he says. "But I don't know if I want to find out."

I ignore his statement and turn my attention to the bags he's carrying.

"I hope you've got something edible with you," I say, then add, "and who in the hell are those banshees out there?"

▼

Riley does not disappoint. He's brought back the best cup of coffee I've ever had in my life—just the way I love it: black and medium-strong. But the best part is what he brought back in the white paper sack—the most delectable, buttery, tender scones in the universe. And if there's one thing I adore more than a grilled cheese sandwich, it's a perfect scone—only I've never had one until now.

I have no idea how Riley seems to know all my likes and dislikes, but I'm starting to enjoy it. Who wouldn't? The only damper on the whole breakfast experience is the incessant chanting outside.

After I explain what happened to my hair, Riley keeps insisting that I tell him the name of the actress whose husband attacked me. When I refuse and won't budge, he finally drops it.

"Do you want me to trim it for you?" he asks.

"Pardon me?"

"I cut my own hair," he says. "I don't trust barbers."

I think of romantic films where the man washes the woman's hair—*Out of Africa* comes to mind—but while this situation is feeling more and more romantic, I'm not sure I trust Riley enough to let him near me with a pair of scissors.

"I need to get going soon," I say. "If I have to listen to that chanting much longer, I'm going to lose a few million more brain cells."

Riley checks his watch. As he does, I pull his wrist toward me so I can see the time. It's a few minutes before nine.

"They'll be finished soon," Riley says.

"You mean, they do this every day?"

"Every day so far," he tells me.

"I hope you got this place cheap," I say.

Riley goes into the bedroom and comes back with a small black case. He unzips it and reveals a mini barber kit—scissors, electric shaver, and other implements.

He takes a dishtowel from the kitchen and ties it around my neck in the back.

"Relax," he says and presses on my shoulders.

"I want to look in the mirror while you cut it," I say.

"No peeking," he replies. "You have to trust me."

"Aren't you even going to ask me how I want it cut?"

"With this kind of damage, your choices are limited, Dakota."

And so he starts to clip and snip, snip and clip. I feel hair falling all around me, like needles drifting from a pine tree. Riley isn't the kind of barber who chats while he clips. He gives the assignment his full concentration and doesn't say a word. The only good part is that the chanting has stopped—cut off cold, as if someone had pulled the plug on a radio.

"See, told you," he says.

"He speaks," I reply.

"I don't want to get distracted and cut left when I meant to cut right."

"So who are the chanters?"

"Can we talk about it after I finish?"

"When will you be finished?"

"Be right back," he says, then sets down his scissors and leaves the room. He returns with a manila envelope and hands it to me.

"You can read while I cut," he tells me.

I flip through the material and get the gist of it—a variety of alien-encounter cults thrive in Southern California.

"So those chanters are communicating with aliens," I say.

"That's what I understand," Riley says.

"And you've been researching these groups for a while."

When Riley doesn't respond, I repeat the question.

"Oh, sorry," he says, "I nodded."

"And since my back is turned, I couldn't see it," I tell him. He sets down his scissors.

"Here," he says, handing me a mirror with a handle.

Oooh, it's short—a pixie cut. I haven't worn my hair this short since . . . I've never worn my hair this short. He did a good job . . . did as much as he could do with my effed-up hair.

I nod and smile, then say, "Don't let me forget to give you a tip."

He puts his finger on my chin and tilts it up, looking into my face as if seeing me for the first time.

"Now we match," he says, putting his hands up to his bald head.

I put my hands up to my head and feel my lack of hair. Yes, I do feel nearly bald.

"Well, thanks," I say.

"Any time."

He puts his hands on my upper arms and pulls me toward him. Just then, I think of something, taking a step back, folding my arms and staring at him.

"Don't tell me it was a coincidence that you rented a place where people hold alien encounter meetings."

"I didn't say it was."

"You told me you found this sublet on Craigslist."

"I did."

"But you'd been here before at one of the alien meetings."

"I left that part out."

"Do you really believe in alien encounters?"

"Something is happening, Dakota. I'm just trying to find out what it is."

"You think somebody wanted to kill you into silence?"

"I don't think. I'm sure. Didn't I die once already?"

"This is all too strange for me, Riley. I don't want to believe in any of it."

"It's not your story," he says. "It's mine."

"So do you buy the theory that Milton's photos don't show any alien visitations, and were just a practical joke?"

"I'd like to take another look at the pictures," he says.

"I might be able to arrange that," I tell him.

◀ TWENTY-FIVE ▶

Before leaving the bungalow, Riley ties the blue bandana around my head and puts the Ray-Bans on my face. He also sets a fedora over my pixie cut and tells me to keep my head down.

"If anyone stops us," he says, "I'll say you've injured your eye and I'm taking you to the ophthalmologist. Okay?"

"You're writing this masterpiece," I reply. I can't see his face, but I have the impression Riley's smiling.

We make it to the car without incident, and Riley buckles me into my seat. Then he leans down and gives me a light kiss on the lips.

"Thank you," he says.

I'm not sure what he's thanking me for, but get the impression that he thinks I've been a good sport . . . something like that, anyway.

The car takes off, and I lean back for the blindfolded drive.

"What time is it?" I ask.

"What time do you think it is?"

"I told you I have a nonexistent sense of time."

"Take a guess."

"Well, the chanters left around nine, then we ate breakfast, you cut my hair, we reviewed the material on the alien encounter groups, and talked for a while. Is it noon?"

"It's 11:15."

Riding blindfolded is a strange experience because you're not anticipating what's ahead—the stoplights, the road signs, the traffic. You just let yourself float along, as if you and the car are one. Now I know why I always loved playing Pin the Tail on the Donkey.

The longer I experience the feeling, the more I enjoy it. It's like letting someone else drive magnified a hundred times— letting go and just accepting what's happening in the moment. Riding blindfolded is sinking into a place where you experience what is, not what you expect things to be. I feel my mind quiet down, then ideas start to flood into my head.

"How much longer?" I ask.

"I thought you'd fallen asleep," Riley says.

"Not quite," I say.

"Another twenty minutes," he tells me.

"Do you know where I can buy a DNA test?" I ask.

"Where did that come from?"

"This blindfold has put me in kind of a trance. I'm getting all kinds of ideas. Things are clicking."

"Let me in on it," he says.

"I will, eventually," I tell him.

"You can buy DNA tests on the Internet."

"I mean someplace where you can walk in and buy one. Aren't there labs that use them?"

"I'd suggest Koreatown," he says. "You can find everything there."

A while later—I'm not sure how long—Riley pulls into a parking spot. He asks me to lean my head down while I remove the Ray-Bans and blindfold. When I do, the sunlight blinds me and I have to put my hands over my eyes.

"Oooh, that hurts," I say.

I feel Riley slip the sunglasses onto my face. I take a deep breath and stare through the dark green lenses onto the dark green world of Olympic Boulevard just west of Westwood. We're parked behind my Toyota, which, thank God, is still there—and I don't see a ticket on the windshield as I stare through the car's back window.

I turn to Riley and say, "So how can I reach you?"

"Here," he says, pressing a piece of paper into my hand. I look down and see a phone number.

"It's one of those disposable phones," he says. "Untraceable."

"What's next?" I ask.

"I'm making it up as I go along," he tells me.

"I'll call you," I say and get out of the car.

"I want to see those photographs," he says before I close the door. "I'm going to hold you to that."

"I'll try to set something up for tomorrow."

"Where?"

"For the time being, let's keep that a surprise."

▼

I don't drink coffee that often, so feel supercharged from the gourmet brew that Riley brought me this morning. As I start to head east on Olympic, it occurs to me that it's lunchtime—and I can do some nearby recon.

I turn left on Westwood, which I take to Wilshire and turn right. In a few minutes, I'm in Beverly Hills, making a tour of the main drags—keeping my eye out for Shelly Morris, aka Shelby Norris. Joyce told me she's seen Shelly trolling the hills of Beverly scamming lunchtime repasts at local feeding troughs.

As I putter along in traffic, I take in the Beverly Hills vibe—Disneyland as imagined by Salvador Dali. I can envision the surrealist's portrait of the place—dripping diamonds, melting gold, and crumbling masks. If you've ever wondered where they get pictures for badplasticsurgery.com, it's the ladies who lunch in Beverly Hills.

While I weave through the streets of 90210, I think the same thing over and over. *Where are you, Shelly? Where are you? I need to talk to you. I'm not mad about you walking out on the lunch check. I just want to talk to you.*

When I'm about to give up and make my way home, I spot my target entering Luciano's, a storefront bistro that proclaims "Grand Opening Week." Yes, Shelly is going to try her tricks on some new, unsuspecting victims—and it appears that she's partial to Italian cuisine.

The fates are with me—just a half a block away, someone pulls out of a parking space and I pull in. When I check the meter, there are ninety-eight minutes remaining. I slide in two more quarters just in case I can convince Shelly to speak to me for the next two hours.

I enter Luciano's—a cute bistro like so many other quaint eateries: white tablecloths, big bottles of olive oil, waiters in white shirts, black pants, and bow ties—and scan the room but don't see Shelly. Did she escape in the brief time it took me to park the car? Is she in the ladies' room?

When the host asks if he can seat me, I tell him I'm meeting someone, then offer a description of Shelly Morris. He nods and leads me through the restaurant to an outdoor patio. And there she is—sitting in a cream silk suit under a bottle-green umbrella. Her face rests on her hand, and she appears to be dozing.

"Your party has arrived," the host says to Shelly, whose eyes get wide when she sees me. The host does a combination bow/nod and glides away.

I see her eyes dart toward the exit and her hand grab her purse. I try to think of something intriguing enough to make her want to stick around and talk.

"Pauline Granton sends her regards," I say.

Shelly leans back and starts to shake, as if someone has electrified her wrought-iron chair.

"Good God," she says, then covers her face with her hands.

I pull out a chair and sit down.

▼

Thirty minutes later, the preliminaries are out of the way and the food is on the table. I've explained how Pauline identified her in a photo. I've also reassured Shelly that I'm not upset about the lunchtime scam she pulled on me earlier in the week.

After my preamble, Shelly looks relaxed and raring to eat. And, unlike our last encounter when I was suffering from a serious migraine, this time I am headache-free and ravenous. Yes, the Milton Kingman project just keeps ringing up expenses, but I figure I'll save money in the long run if Shelly can provide some missing pieces of the puzzle—and prevent me from following blind leads.

While eating, we exchange light chatter about Pauline Granton and her husband. I mention that Albert suffers from

Alzheimer's and spends a good part of each day reliving the sci-fi and horror scripts he wrote for Duke Galveston. To give Shelly the sense that I'm sharing a bit of a secret—and try to gain her trust—I tell her the story of how Albert attacked me with scissors and hacked off my hair.

"You look better in short hair," Shelly says, swirling linguini carbonara around her fork.

"This is the amended version," I say, pointing to my hair.

"Anyway, Albert has a scissors fixation," Shelly says. "He wrote a scissors attack somewhere in each of his scripts. I asked him once where the aliens got the scissors and he told me 'telekinesis.'"

"I guess telekinesis could serve as the answer to any question," I offer.

"Albert's father was a tailor," Shelly says. "I think the scissors thing goes back to his childhood."

I'm glad to see that Shelly is engaged in our conversation. I figure it's a good time to slide in some of the topics I want to discuss.

"When I was at Pauline's house, she pointed out an actress named Geraldine Bright in some of the photos."

Shelly sits up straight with such a stiff back that when her head moves she looks like a Bobblehead. I wait for her to say something. After a full minute, I repeat the question.

"I heard you the first time," she tells me. "I prefer not to answer."

"Please, Shelly," I say in my most placating and pleading voice—one that's just on the verge of begging. "It's important."

Shelly pushes her half-full plate away. Now I know she's upset.

"Why is it important?" she asks.

I have to decide how much I want to tell her—whether to give her the barest details and hope she'll take the bait or if I need to share the full story.

She crosses her arms, throws on a pair of Jackie O sunglasses, and starts to click her heel on the cement patio. I know there's no way around it. I'll have to tell her everything and share all my suspicions.

▼

An hour later, Shelly and I are in my car headed for Pauline Granton's place in Bel Air. During our conversation at the restaurant, she'd cleared up a lot of the mystery surrounding Milton Kingman, his wife Geraldine, and Shelly's former love Duke Galveston. Now she's agreed to accompany me as I try to solve another enigma.

On the way, we stop at a Rite-Aid and pick up something we'll need to learn the truth about a long-standing secret.

"I saw you at the Beverly Hilton bar a couple of nights ago," I say.

"I know," she replies. "You were with that blonde woman, the one who sells her drawings."

"That's Joyce," I say. "She said she could help me find you."

Shelly doesn't respond. She knows where this conversation is headed—that I'm trying to get her to admit she's homeless. Her mind works fast, and she anticipates my every move. There's no way I can outsmart her.

I glance at my passenger. Her manicured hands are folded in serene repose in the lap of her silk suit. She knows she doesn't look like a homeless woman—and will continue to play the part she's dressed for: a wealthy widow. I decide not to take this any further and change the subject.

"Pauline is looking forward to seeing you," I tell Shelly, mentioning what she'd told me on the phone when I called to ask if we could stop by.

"How does she look?" Shelly asks. This is probably the question any woman would ask about a friend she hasn't seen in over fifty years.

"Beautiful," I say.

Shelly nods and smiles. "Pauline was always a lovely woman. And smart. She was practically the only one of us who didn't get involved with Duke."

▼

After I pull into Pauline Granton's driveway, Shelly tells me to wait while she freshens her lipstick and powders her nose. When we get out of the car, she straightens her blouse, smoothes her skirt, then crunches across the gravel driveway in her beige Ferragamo pumps, shoulders high, back straight, head held high.

Before we get to the front walk, the door flings open and Pauline rushes down the stairs toward Shelly, giving her a heartfelt hug.

▼

Pauline and Shelly spend the next few hours catching up—chatting, drinking coffee, and looking at photographs from Pauline's collection. When I ask if I can tape their conversation for research purposes, they agree—after I promise to check with them before including any of their reminiscences in Milton's book. I assure them I'll only use the material as background, but something else occurs to me—because I'm always thinking about my next assignment.

"Maybe one or both of you would like to write your memoirs."

Shelly doesn't answer, but Pauline replies, "I can't write."

"That's how I can help," I say.

Pauline beams at me and says, "We'll see."

I wait for Shelly to make a trip to the restroom before explaining to Pauline the main reason for my visit. As I speak, the brilliant smile fades and the skin tightens over her high cheekbones.

"But why dredge this all up now?" she asks. "It can only cause pain."

"It can offer closure for some of the people involved," I say.

Pauline closes her eyes, takes in a long breath, and then exhales with a sound that sounds like "aah." As Shelly walks back into the room, Pauline nods at me and says, "Go ahead."

▼

When I pull out of Pauline's driveway, I check my dashboard clock. It's just after six. A few minutes earlier, Pauline had invited us to stay for dinner, but I'd told her I needed to work. Using the tact of a consummate diplomat, Pauline had asked Shelly to do her a favor and spend a few days at the house—never letting on that she knew Shelly is homeless.

While driving away, I feel relieved that Pauline spared me the guilt I'd have felt dumping Shelly back on the streets of Beverly Hills.

As I drive, I try to plan my next few moves. I've been making decisions on the fly since getting into Riley's car yesterday, but now I need to think things through.

Thirty minutes later, I'm on Milton's doorstep, but still not sure what to say. The bottom line: Milton Kingman is my client, so I have to be honest with him. I can't commit a sin of omission—not telling him the real reason for my visit and leading him to believe my motives are different from what they really are.

When Milton answers the door, he says, "Dakota" and nods, as if he'd anticipated my arrival. He steps aside to let me walk through the door. I don't have time to ease into this, so just blurt out my request. "I need to talk to Conrad," I say. "Can you give me his phone number?"

"He won't bother you anymore," Milton says, patting me on the shoulder. "Don't worry."

"It's something else," I say.

After I explain my reasons, he says, "I'll tell you under one condition."

Somehow I know what he's going to say, but I ask anyway. "What's that?"

"I want to go with you."

◀ TWENTY-SIX ▶

I almost change my mind when Milton tells me that Conrad lives in Redondo Beach. In rush hour, it'll take at least an hour to get there on the streets. I consider postponing the meeting until the following afternoon, but figure something might come up to prevent the trip—so I'd better do it now.

"Do you think he's at home?" I ask.

"I'll call and find out," Milton says.

"Okay," I say. "If he's at his place, tell him to stick around and expect an important delivery. If he asks you what, just say it's a surprise."

Milton nods and heads toward the phone.

"Do you think he'll go for it?" I ask. "I mean, are you on speaking terms?"

"Everything is status quo," he says. "Don't worry, I can handle it."

And he does—placing the call and telling Conrad everything I'd asked him to say. After he hangs up, Milton says, "I was just about to eat. Mind if I grab a bite before we take off?"

"Do you get carsick?" I say.

"I don't travel in a car very much these days."

"I mean, it might not be a good idea to eat and go for a long drive."

"I'll just have a couple of frozen waffles," he says, then adds: "Want some? They're Eggos."

"Something light would hit the spot," I say. "I had a big lunch."

▼

At a little before seven by my dashboard clock, we're in my car heading south on Lincoln Boulevard. It's still bright out, but the light is fading, making the world on the other side of the windshield look like an overexposed photo. I turn on my headlights because it'll be nearly dark by the time we reach our destination.

As I drive, I glance over at Milton from time to time and think how small and vulnerable he looks—like a young child strapped into the seat. I'm tempted to stop and ask him to sit in the back, where you're supposed to place children to prevent them from getting hurt during an accident.

Milton's hands are on the dashboard and his head is near the windshield, aiming for the best view of the stream of life—his cataracts smoothing out all the hard edges. He looks happy, his face lit up with a big grin.

As time passes, the sky pales to a hazy violet. The traffic slows as we approach LAX, but I don't really mind because it gives me a chance to watch planes float through the twilight sky as they land and take off. I imagine myself on an Air France jet as it rises in the air.

Lincoln Blvd. turns into Sepulveda and we enter a long tunnel—one that's appeared in scores of movies. The traffic inches along, so it's not a driving hazard to read the graffiti scrawled on the walls. I'm not as interested in the messages as much as imagining how someone managed to walk into this busy tunnel and paint on the concrete walls. That's a dedicated artist for you.

When I hear Milton yawn, I ask him if he's okay.

"Fine. Fine," he says. "Enjoying the ride."

"What time do you usually go to bed?" I ask. I look at the dashboard clock. It's 7:35.

"Oh, around ten," he replies. "I'm fine."

"Do you want to stop for coffee in El Segundo?" I ask, mentioning the town on the other end of the tunnel.

"Let's just keep going," he says.

"Do you want to listen to the radio?" I ask.

"If you want to turn it on, do it," he tells me.

I punch on KUSC-FM, 91.5, the classical station, and they're playing the perfect music for a sunset drive—Erik Satie's Gymnopedie No. 3 on classical guitar.

"Do you have enough gas?" Milton asks.

I check the gauge. "I've got enough to get us to Redondo Beach and back to your place."

"How much?" he asks.

"Abut a third of a tank," I tell him.

"Stop at a station and fill up," he says.

"I thought you wanted to keep going."

"If there's one thing I can stand, it's going on a long trip without a full tank of gas."

"It's not really a long trip."

"For me it is."

We make it to the other side of the tunnel just as the last notes sound to Satie's masterwork.

"Did you enjoy that?" I ask.

"Enjoy what?"

"The music."

"Didn't notice," he says. "I was worrying about the gas."

Well, I think to myself, somebody's got to think about the practical stuff—it sure as hell isn't me.

After the pit stop, where Milton visited the restroom, he finally seems to relax as we travel south, Sepulveda turning into Pacific Coast Highway. The car windows are open and the sea breeze wafts in—one of my favorite aromas, better than any cologne. The air feels misty and my Midwestern pores are jumping up and cheering—thinking we're back home where it rains more than a few inches a year.

"Sorry to be like that," Milton says.

"Like what?"

"Insisting that you stop for gas," he tells me.

"Well, you did pay for it."

"It's just that I get so nervous without a full tank," he says. "And it's all Duke's doing."

Great, I think, Milton is remembering an anecdote. Maybe if I drive him around for a week or so, I'll get enough material for the book.

"What happened?" I ask, but Milton doesn't answer.

As we drive through Manhattan Beach, I look to my right and get a glimpse of the Pacific, feeling my heart open up. Every time I'm near the ocean, I vow to visit more often, but it's a long drive from where I live, and I usually don't want to use up that much gas for a joy ride. But tonight I promise my-self to spend more time near this body of water that I love so much.

My proximity to the ocean and the imminent sundown has put me in a mellow mood. I want to enhance the feeling with more music, but Milton starts to talk when I'm about to click on the radio.

"You know that Duke was an aviator," he says. When I nod, he continues. "Well, I didn't like flying with him, and he knew it. But he was forever finding reasons for us to fly someplace. Had me sit in the copilot seat so I could watch the gas go down, down, down to almost nothing. He knew it drove me crazy. More than once, we were in the air when the plane sputtered out of gas, and Duke had to glide to a landing in some field. We were lucky we didn't get killed."

Milton inhales, then shudders as he exhales, his shoulders rising above his ears. The air feels chilly and moist. I roll up the windows so Milton won't start to shiver.

I decide that it's a perfect moment to bring up a delicate subject—and get Milton's mind going in a certain direction.

"I understand that Duke was quite a practical joker," I say.

"He played the running-out-of-gas trick on me more than once."

"Any other practical jokes?"

"I saw him pull stunts on other people."

"Like what?"

"I don't know if you'd call it a joke. More like mean tricks."

I remember what Pauline had told me—that Duke took Shelly Morris on a ship and got a fake captain to marry them—his way of tricking her into giving up her virginity. I assume that Shelly wasn't the only woman Duke took advantage of in one way or another.

"I wonder why you remained friends with Duke for so long," I say.

Milton puts his hands on his knees and sits up straight. When I turn to glance at him, his cloudy eyes are open wide, as if trying to see into the past.

"We were in business together," Milton answers. "I wouldn't say we were ever really friends."

"Then why do you want to write this book about him?"

"I just feel the story needs to get out. People have a right to know about this. I want to put this down on paper before I die."

"Besides the running out of gas, what other kinds of practical jokes did Duke pull on you?"

"He'd say he was going out of town on business," Milton replies. "But then I'd find out he didn't go anywhere and had disguised himself as a gaffer or grip, just so he could spy on me and see how I was handling things in his absence."

"Anything else?"

"All kinds of stuff," Milton replies. "I don't feel like talking about it anymore."

Milton bends down and looks through the window at the darkening sky.

"Looking for UFOs?" I ask, hoping he'll laugh—but he doesn't.

"When the UFO crashed in Roswell back in 1947," Milton tells me, "Duke was called in to look at the vehicle and the alien corpses. He told me about it many, many times."

"And the government called on him because . . ."

"He was the most famous aviator in the world. He designed airplanes. There was nobody else who knew as much about aircraft as Duke Galveston."

"So these other aliens," I say, "the aliens that you met, were they related to the ones that crashed at Roswell?"

"Turn here," Milton says, pointing to the sign arching across the roadway: Redondo Beach King Harbor.

As the car glides under the archway, Milton looks up at the words written there, and says "King" out loud.

"Any relation, Mr. Kingman?" I say, as I wind down Catalina Avenue, past streets named for precious gems.

Milton smiles and says, "Every time I see the word 'king,' I think it relates to me. It's odd, but over the years I've worked with quite a few people with royal-type names. Let's see. There was Charlie Prince. There was Earl Reynolds. Sally Knight. That's Knight with a 'kn.' And, oh yes, Billy McQueen and Miranda Lord."

"And there was Duke Galveston," I say.

"This is it. Turn here," Milton says, pointing to an apartment building fronting the ocean.

I make a right into a lot and pull into a spot marked "guest parking."

"Are you up for this?" I ask.

"It's been a long time coming," he says.

I help Milton out of the car and steady him as we walk down the sloping driveway to the main gate, where we both stare at the name "Kingman" next to the doorbell. We look at each other as if trying to decide which one of us should announce our arrival. After a few seconds, Milton sticks out his arthritis-swollen index finger and presses the white doorbell.

While we wait, I gaze through the white-grill fence to the ocean about a hundred yards away, letting the breeze wash over me, and taking in the final strands of sunlight on the water. Milton wobbles on his feet and I clasp his elbow to steady him. A voice comes over the intercom.

"Who is it?" It's Conrad, and he sounds frantic—as if this intrusion is the final blow sending him over the edge.

"It's me," Milton says.

"Dad?" Conrad asks, managing to draw out the word so it sounds like "Daaaaaaaaddddddd??????"

"Yes," Milton replies. "Open up."

◀ TWENTY-SEVEN ▶

While we wait, I let the breeze move through my pixie hair-cut. I've never felt the air directly on my head this way, and it's an odd sensation, as if the wind is passing through my skull and eliminating everything I don't need—all the mindless drivel that eats up most of my time. I feel awake and refreshed.

"Are you cold?" I ask Milton.

"Not at all," he says. "How about you?"

"I'm surprised that it's still so warm, especially right next to the ocean."

"It's been ages since I walked along the beach," he tells me. "I can't remember the last time. Before I die, I want to take off my shoes and walk in the sand."

"I'll drive you to Santa Monica next week," I say.

"No," he responds, "not next week. Now! I want to walk on the beach tonight. Who knows how much longer I'll live? It's a perfect evening. Might as well make the most of it."

I see Conrad exit a five-story white brick apartment building. If I had to pick one adjective to describe him, it would be "seething." He's a big man, but his rage makes him appear even taller and wider, as if he is filling up with some kind of toxic gas.

He is so irate that his capacity for speech is gone, his mouth trying to form a word, any word. Finally, he points at me through the metal gate and says, "You!"

He bangs into the gate, as if forgetting that he has to open it before walking through. In his inarticulate clumsiness, Conrad reminds me of Frankenstein's monster—only not as attractive or charming. He fumbles with the lock, and after more than a few attempts slams open the gate and lunges toward me. Milton intervenes, putting himself between us.

"Get out of our way," Milton says. "We're going for a walk on the beach."

Milton nudges Conrad aside, having as much effect as a sparrow trying to move the Rock of Gibraltar. Conrad turns and watches as Milton rushes down the stone pathway toward the ocean. He forgets about me and follows his Daaaaaddddd.

"You mean you came all the way out here to walk on the beach?" Conrad says, catching up with Milton and trying to stop him by pulling on both shoulders.

Milton is used to this move, dipping out of Conrad's grip and speeding down the walkway as if propelled by some kind of supernatural force. I remember that Milton has left his cane in the car, but figure if he stumbles, the sand should break his fall.

"Daaadddd! Daaaadddddd!" Conrad calls, stumbling after Milton down the walkway lit by dim ground lights.

Milton has scrambled ahead, beyond the lights and into the darkness of the beach and the wall of ocean beyond it.

"Daaddd!" Conrad calls. "Where are you?"

I trail behind father and son and have the feeling that this evening will never end. I can't see how it will come to any conclusion. I'll just keep walking up and down a darkened beach for all eternity looking for Milton and trying to avoid a confrontation with Conrad. This is my fatalistic streak coming to the surface—and, at some point in every writing gig, it appears. All seems bleak, hopeless, pointless.

I take a step from the lighted path into the darkness. I hear no voices—just the sound of the waves whooshing against the sand.

Where is Milton? Where is Conrad? A terrifying thought crosses my mind: *What if they were abducted by aliens?* A dark, lonely beach at night is just the kind of place I'd imagine as an abduction spot. Oh, God, how I wish I were home. I say a "Hail Mary," and I'm not sure if I'm reciting it in my head or speaking out loud.

I think of running back to my car and driving away, but I can't do it. I need to follow through with the reason for this visit—and I can't abandon Milton out here. But where is he?

As I walk toward the water, I glance to my left and my right, but can't make out anything. I look in the sky and my heart jolts. I think I see a huge silver disc hovering there, and my legs give out under me.

I fall to my knees and cover my face with my hands. I don't want to look, but I have to. Yes, it's a silvery disc, but not a UFO. It's the moon rising above the horizon—and I've never before seen such a huge moon. It's nightmare scary. Yes, at this point, I'm so far gone and so freaked that I'm afraid of the moon.

I hear a murmur of voices, like the low rumble of an engine, and turn to my right. I see two figures coming toward me, dark silhouettes against a lighter sky.

I fumble in my bag for my penlight, which I haven't used since I hid in Milton's closet trying to avoid Conrad. My hand feels the cold metal, and I pray that the batteries haven't gone dead. I pull out the flashlight and aim it at the approaching shadows.

"Right in my eye!" shouts a blond teenager with his arm around a surfboard.

"Sorry," I say, clicking off the light, then asking, "Did you see anyone else around here?"

"I just got out," he says, moving away. The way he says the words, he could mean he just got out of jail or a mental institution—but I know he's telling me he just stepped out of the ocean.

As I sit in the cool sand, with the huge moon hovering over me, I feel an overwhelming sense of isolation, as if I'm stranded on a desert island. I want to talk to someone, anyone, and look in the direction where the surfer moved, but he's evaporated into the night.

It occurs to me that my phone hasn't rung all day, and I remember it's set on mute. I grab the phone out of my bag, and find that I have both voicemail and text messages. It's now 8:32. At 8:07, Marelle texted that Ryan was at her place and would wait for another hour. The detective isn't sure when he can contact me again.

As I dial voicemail, I listen to the water moving against the shore and feel a warm breeze blow through my shorn head. I take deep breaths and try to absorb the moment, my surroundings, everything except that scary-looking moon floating in the sky and on the ocean.

I have ten messages—several from people who've called more than once. Detective Hernandez wants to talk to me about Riley Taylor's fatal traffic accident. Riley Taylor wants to know when he can review the Milton Kingman file—and called a few more times to find out how I was and tell me he was looking forward to seeing me again.

I reach in my pocket and pull out the piece of paper where Riley wrote his phone number. I aim my penlight at the paper and dial. He picks up on the first ring.

"Where are you?" he answers.

"Redondo Beach."

"Why?"

"I drove Milton out here to see his son."

"The son who reported you to the cops?"

"Detective Hernandez called again today and left messages."

"I thought you said they found sonny's complaint groundless."

"That's not why L.A.'s finest wants to talk to me."

"Oh," Riley says. "It has something to do with me."

"I was the last known person to have seen you before the accident."

"Sorry, Dakota," he says. "Just tell them what happened that night."

"I did. But you know how detectives are. They keep interviewing you, hoping you'll remember a new detail, or slip up and admit something."

"I'm sorry I got you mixed up in this."

"They're not buying that we just met a few days before your crash."

"Let them investigate you," he says. "They won't find anything."

"I'd better go. I have to look for Milton and Conrad."

"Where are they now?"

"Milton wanted to walk on the beach and Conrad ran after him. I don't know where they are."

"Where are you?"

"Sitting in the sand."

"Alone?"

"There's a very full moon keeping me company."

"Sounds romantic, but a little dangerous."

"Just how I like it," I say.

"Seriously, I think you should get out of there."

"Afraid I'll be abducted by aliens?"

"It's happened before."

"If it has, I don't recall."

"Just get in your car and leave."

"I promised to take Milton home."

"Does this visit have anything to do with that DNA test you were talking about?"

"It might."

Someone yanks the phone out of my hand and growls, "I'm gonna put you behind bars yet."

I can't see him, but I recognize the voice as Conrad's. I notice a shorter shadow next to his.

"Come on, Dakota. Let's go," Milton says.

"What have you been telling my Dad?" Conrad whines.

"Conrad, I'm only trying to help."

"You're taking advantage of my father, and now you're trying to take advantage of me," he accuses.

"Please give me back my phone," I say.

"Here," Conrad replies, and I see his shadow move and then hear a soft thud in the sand. "Find it!" he screeches.

The phone is still lit up because I didn't hang up from the call to Riley—and I assume he's still on the other end of the line. For all his height and heft, Conrad isn't a very good throw—the phone landed just a few feet away. I pick it up and listen.

"Still there?" I ask.

"Want me to drive out and kick his ass?" Riley asks.

"I'll call you when I get home," I say.

"No," he tells me. "Call me on the way home."

"Later," I say and click off.

I catch up with Milton and Conrad on the path leading to the parking lot.

"Did you take your shoes off and walk on the sand?" I ask.

"Certainly," Milton replies. "A moonlight stroll. I only wish Geraldine were with me. But I imagined she was."

I unlock the car and help Milton into the passenger seat. When I approach the driver's side, Conrad is sitting on my fender, and he makes a fake lunge toward me. I stand my ground and stare him down—his face glowing a greenish yellow in the sodium vapor lights.

"You came all the way out here for nothing," he growls.

"Why did I come out here?"

"My Dad told me."

"And what was that?"

"He thinks I took some of his memorabilia and sold it on eBay. He came out here to get it back."

"I know why you're buying and selling stuff on eBay, and I know what you're looking for," I tell him.

He sneers and says, "You don't know shit."

"I know you're looking for a piece of Duke Galveston so you can test your DNA against his and make a claim on the billons he left to medical research."

"None of this is your business," he says, his shoulders hunched over and his head hanging low.

"But I have what you're looking for."

He lifts his head and shifts his eyes to the side: a look that's cautious but with a flicker of hope.

Rather than respond, he mumbles something—and while the words aren't discernible, the meaning is clear: "Oh yeah?"

I give him the short version—explaining that I'd interviewed Duke Galveston's one-time common law wife who gave me a strand of hair from the lock she carries with her. I tell him if he'll allow me to take a swab of his cheek, I'll have the DNA tested and give him the results.

"Just give me the hair," he says, jumping up and trying to grab the bag from my shoulder.

"It's locked in a safe," I say, pulling my bag away.

I turn and look into the car and see that Milton is asleep, his mouth hanging open and his chin resting on his chest.

And so with his adoptive father dozing in the passenger seat, Conrad opens his mouth like a baby bird and allows me to take two swabs of his inner cheek. I explain that the second swab is to rule out someone else—and I can see he assumes I'm talking about Milton Kingman. I figure it's best at this point to let him keep thinking that way.

◀ TWENTY-EIGHT ▶

It's a quiet drive back to Brentwood with Milton asleep next to me. I don't mind driving when I'm not in a hurry to get anywhere or make it to an appointment during rush hour. I'm enjoying gliding down the roadways, alternating between the blackness and the streetlights lighting up patches of night. The only thing to make the experience more pleasant would be some classical music. But I don't want to wake up Milton.

The long drive gives me plenty of time to think—something I haven't had a chance to do all day. I dread contacting Detective Hernandez and evading his questions about Riley Taylor. I'm a terrible liar, and he's a good detective who'll figure out I'm trying to hide something. I wonder how long Riley will continue his death charade.

As if he knows I'm thinking about him, my cell phone beeps with a text message. I glance at the phone and see R U OK? At the stoplight, I text back OK LATER. I pull over to the curb and text Ryan, asking the private detective where he is and when I can see him. I wait for a few minutes in case he texts back. The next thing I know, someone is banging on the window.

I look up and see a man in brown—a member of the L.A. County Sheriff's Department—at my side window. I have no idea how much time has passed since I fell asleep. I roll down my window a few inches. Milton is still zonked out—at least I hope he's asleep.

"Is everyone all right?" the fresh-faced blond officer says. He looks young enough to be my son.

"Yes, officer," I say.

"What happened?" he asks, ducking down to see inside the car.

"I pulled over to use the phone," I answer, "and I must have dozed off for a moment."

"Is the gentleman all right?"

I turn to Milton and nudge his shoulder. He lets out a sputtering snore.

"It's been a long day," I say. "I'm driving him back to Brentwood."

"Your grandfather?" he says.

I feel flattered that the officer doesn't think Milton is my father. I must look well rested after that nice little nap.

"My client."

"Are you an attorney?"

I'm flattered that the officer thinks I look smart enough to be an attorney. I must look mentally sharp after that nice little nap.

"Ghostwriter," I say. "I'm helping Mr. Kingman with his memoirs. We were visiting his son in Redondo Beach."

The officer takes a step back, as if something has just occurred to him. He scans my car from front to back. I know what he's thinking: Why am I driving such an old vehicle if I'm an upstanding professional?

"Step out of the car," he says.

I've seen too many movies where the cops think you're trying to pull a gun if they can't see your hands, so I put my hands above my head as the officer opens the door and lets me out.

"Stand by the curb," he says.

He reaches into the car and pulls out my bag, rummaging through it until he finds my wallet. After pulling out my license and insurance card, he heads for the patrol car. He seems excited, as if imagining all the glory he'll get for a big-time bust.

I have no idea what time it is as I stand on Lincoln Blvd., about a block past Maxella. I should have never stopped to send that text message.

I want to ask the officer if I can get a sweater out of the car, but figure that's not a good idea. I'm starting to shake from cold and fear, and try to stop myself from spiraling into panic. What do I have to be afraid of? It's not like I've done anything wrong or I'm wanted by the police.

Cars whiz by, some drivers rubbernecking to see the male-factor standing next to the patrol car, trying to imagine what I could have done to get pulled over.

I close my eyes and let the night air seep into me. After a few minutes, I hear someone banging on glass. I look at the car and see that Milton is awake and trying to open the door. The officer exits the patrol car and approaches Milton's side of the car. He pulls open the door and says, "Who is this woman?" pointing to me.

Milton blinks a few times and responds, "I have no idea."

"Put your hands behind your back," the officer tells me as he approaches with a set of handcuffs.

"Officer," I say, "Mr. Kingman just woke up. I'm sure he's somewhat disoriented." I look at Milton and say, "Four thousand bucks."

Milton squinches his eyes tight, then opens them wide.

"Where am I? What's going on, Dakota?" he says, just as the man in the brown shirt is about to give me a new set of bracelets.

"I was driving you home and pulled over," I tell Milton. "The officer stopped to see if we were okay."

"What time is it?" Milton asks.

"Sit in the car, sir," the officer instructs.

"I need to use the restroom," Milton replies.

A few minutes later, Milton and I are in the back seat of the patrol car on our way to the nearest sheriff's department station—so that Milton can use the restroom, or so the officer tells us.

When we pull into the parking lot, I see boats rocking in the nearby harbor. Music and laughter come from some of the vessels—and I wonder how many wild parties get busted. Probably none, because the cops are busy picking up hardened criminals like me.

We climb out of the patrol car and the officer leads us into the Marina del Rey L.A. Sheriff's Department substation. My first thought is that "Rey" means King in Spanish—and I want

187

to mention it to Milton, but figure the fewer words the better at this point.

While Milton uses the facilities, the officer, who looks even younger and blonder under fluorescent lights, tells me to give him my bag, which I hand over. He then directs me into a small room—equipped with a table and four chairs—then closes the door. When I try to turn the knob, I see that it's locked.

The big round clock on the wall tells me it's 12:25—and I laugh at the irony, because this is definitely not Christmas. I sit at the table and rest my head on my folded arms.

I feel someone shaking my shoulder and sit up, blinking and yawning. The clock says 2:14, and I know it's not Valentine's Day. When I look up, I see the officer, whose nametag says "Richards." I felt exhausted and my neck is stiff. God, will this day never end?

"Can we go now?" I ask.

"We've been asked to hold you until morning."

"Hold us why?"

"That's all the information I can divulge at the moment," he says. "Let me show you to your cell."

I know the sheriff's department needs a good reason to hold me—but I'm not about to get anything out of Officer Richards, a laid-back dude who I figure spends his nonworking hours either sleeping or surfing.

Did Conrad say I'd kidnapped his father? Does Detective Hernandez think I fled? Those are those only two reasons serious enough for the cops to hold me overnight—at least I hope it's only overnight.

I'm just too tired right now to fight, and follow the officer to a room with a cot, a pitcher of water, and a toilet. That's all I need at the moment.

Then I'm in the mountains, driving south on treacherous Highway 1. It's getting dark and the traffic is moving faster and faster, and I'm afraid of plunging into the ocean. I try to keep up with the flow of traffic, but car horns are blasting. Then I remember something—I took a sedative and will fall asleep any second. As I speed around a curve and the car starts spinning, I scream myself awake.

When I open my eyes and look around, it takes me nearly a minute to remember where I am. I dread what the morning holds—police interrogations and, if they let me out, a long drive home. I haven't had a shower in two days. I can't stand myself.

I close my eyes and think about the dream I just had—a recurring nightmare. My unconscious has combined two scary incidents involving cars—a trip with my daughter through the mountains, and the time I took an Ambien and woke up sleep driving—and delivers this terrifying scenario to me on a regular basis. I put my hands over my face and take deep breaths, trying to shake the horror I felt in the dream.

A knock at the door makes me sit up and open my eyes. Before I can respond, the door opens and LAPD Detective Hernandez is standing there, looking official in a gray suit, white shirt, and black tie.

"What's for breakfast?" I say, then slide my feet into my shoes.

"Let's go," he says.

"Where's Mr. Kingman?" I say. "Did his son pick him up?"

"I ask the questions," Hernandez says. "You answer them."

"And what do you want to know?" I say as I walk through the door.

"You know what I want to know," he replies.

We make our way to the front desk, where the detective signs a piece of paper and the officer-in-charge hands him a large sack.

"Here," he says, shoving it at me. I look inside and see my bag, phone, and keys.

Hernandez pushes open the front door and saunters over to a late model silver Honda Civic—I wish I had one just like it.

"Get in," he says.

"I need to move my car."

"First, you're going to answer some questions."

I run through a few prayers in my mind, pleading with all the powers in heaven to help me not give myself away. I can't let on that Riley isn't dead—I gave him my word—but the investigative reporter/alien hunter should at least know what's going on.

I slide my cell phone out of my bag—and while Hernandez is getting into the car, hit redial for the last number I called, then ease the phone into my pocket. I figure it won't hurt for the presumed deceased to listen in on this conversation.

As Hernandez cruises past the marina, I gaze at the boats, which look so inviting and peaceful—and I have the feeling that heaven is an endless harbor of blue waters, white sailboats, and pink clouds.

"You should have returned my call yesterday," Hernandez says, putting on a pair of wraparound sunglasses.

"I was busy all day," I said. "I didn't know my phone was on mute."

"Don't you check your messages?"

"It was after ten when I called voicemail."

"You weren't at your apartment the night before last," he says. "And then you don't return my calls for an entire day. What am I supposed to think?"

I know there's only one way out of this situation—to act in the most cooperative, placating manner possible.

"The night before last, I stayed with a friend. Yesterday, I had appointments in Beverly Hills, Bel Air, and Redondo Beach. I was on the road all day."

Hernandez pulls into a parking lot and winds his way around until we're in front of a hotel. I have no idea why we've stopped here.

"I need to talk to you about Riley Taylor," he says.

"I've already told you everything I know."

"Well, let's go over it a few more times. Maybe you'll remember something you forgot."

He opens the car door and gets out, then walks to my side and stands there while I gather my things.

All of a sudden, it dawns on me why we're at this spot. Detective Hernandez is going to buy me breakfast.

▼

It's seven in the morning, but the restaurant is already crowded—all the tourists grabbing a bite before they hit the beaches. After we load up our trays at the breakfast buffet, Hernandez leads me out of the restaurant, down a hallway, and onto a patio facing a pool. It's too early for swimming in an unheated pool, so we have the area all to ourselves.

I wonder if Riley is still on the line and pull my phone out of my pocket as if I want to check the time. When I look at the screen, I act as if a call has just come in.

"Hello," I say.

"I'm still here," Riley says. "Where are you?"

"I should be back by noon," I say, then look to Hernandez, who's getting ready to dig into his steak and eggs. "My catsitter wants to know when I'll be home."

"Depends," Hernandez says.

"Where are you?" Riley asks again.

"On the Westside. It'll take me at least an hour to drive home."

"Where in the hell are you?"

"What's the name of this place?" I ask Hernandez.

"Used to be the Marriott Courtyard."

Riley overhears, then asks, "Marina del Rey?"

"I'm fine. Don't worry," I say, then hang up.

When I sit down and look at my food—an omelet, pancakes, and hash brown potatoes—I'm not hungry, a real switch for me. All I want is coffee, tea, or even cola—anything to help me stay awake.

"Let me see your phone," Hernandez says, then wipes his mouth with a napkin.

I hand him the phone and he checks my incoming calls.

"I guess your catsitter has an untraceable phone," he says.

"Does she?"

"What's the number?" he says.

"Why?"

"I want to talk to her."

"I don't remember the number. She always calls me."

"Who were you really talking to?"

"I told you."

"Guess I'll just have to haul you in. Better eat up, all we have at the station is peanut butter crackers."

"Can I have my phone back?"

"Depends."

"I need to check on Mr. Kingman."

Hernandez hands me the phone. I dial Milton's number, but there's no answer.

"Ambulance took Kingman to the hospital last night."

"Why?"

"Chest pains."

"Take me there. I need to see him."

"If you start answering some questions, I might be able to arrange that."

"What hospital?"

"Right down the street."

I dial directory assistance, but Hernandez grabs the phone away.

"Come on," he says. "While we're there maybe they can analyze the DNA tests in your bag."

The DNA tests! I'd forgotten all about them. I have to send in the samples right away. There's so much to do. And I need a shower!

◀ TWENTY-NINE ▶

During the short ride to the hospital, Detective Hernandez says, "You must know that we saw you make two visits to the site of Riley Taylor's crash."

Before I answer, I try to anticipate where Hernandez is going with this line of questioning. Does he think I was a criminal returning to the scene of the crime? How can I explain why I visited the location? It's complicated. Maybe if I just give him a few facts that he can verify elsewhere he'll stop suspecting me.

Once again, I tell Hernandez how I met Riley when we were both doing research at the Margaret Herrick Library. Riley noticed that I was reviewing material on Duke Galveston and figured out I was working on a book for Milton Kingman—because he, too, had interviewed for the ghostwriting job a few months prior to Kingman hiring me.

On the way home that day, I explain to the detective, I stopped by Duke Galveston's old headquarters at 7000 Iceberg Street. When I started to enter the building, Riley Taylor tapped me on the shoulder and said he needed to talk to me.

"Are you saying he followed you there?" Hernandez asks.

"He left the library before I did," I offer. "I think he knew that I might stop at Galveston's building, based on the notes I was making at the library."

"Go on," Hernandez says as he turns into the hospital parking lot.

"Can we finish this later?" I ask. "I'm worried about Mr. Kingman."

"We'll walk and talk," he replies.

As we make our way toward the hospital entrance, Hernandez says, "So what did Taylor need to talk to you about?"

"Riley became interested in Duke Galveston and started to write his own book, figuring Mr. Kingman had decided not to move forward with his."

While we wait in line at the reception desk, Hernandez says, "So he wanted to talk to you about Duke Galveston?"

"He was surprised that Mr. Kingman was going ahead with his book. I think Riley felt a bit threatened, since he was committed to writing a book on the same subject."

"So why would he think you'd talk about it? Aren't you bound by some kind of confidentiality agreement?"

"And that's just what I told him. That's why we had a few pointed exchanges at the wine bar in West Hollywood."

"But the next night you saw him again," he says.

"That was a case of mistaken identity," I reply.

"How so?"

"I was waiting to hear from a colleague named Ryan. When I received a text message to meet at the Griffith Observatory that was signed R, I thought he was contacting me. It turned out to be Riley Taylor. I was angry that he was badgering me for information about the Duke Galveston book when I'd already told him the day before that I could not and would not breech my confidentiality agreement with Mr. Kingman."

"That still doesn't answer my question," he says.

"What question?"

"Why did you pay two visits to the crash site?"

"The first time, out of curiosity. I was shocked when I read about the accident in the *L.A. Times*. I wanted to see for myself where it happened. I'm a writer. I'm just wired that way."

"And what about the second time?"

"I was driving back from the Westside. It dawned on me to stop at the site to see if people had left messages or placed candles there."

"And had they?"

"You know the answer."

"People are saying it wasn't an accident, that he was murdered," Hernandez says. When I don't respond, he adds, "Isn't that right?"

"Yes."

"Who would have wanted to murder him?"

"He was an investigative reporter. Maybe he was working on a story that put him in danger."

"What kind of story?"

"All I know is what I told you."

"Somehow," Hernandez says, "I'm not buying that."

The line to the reception desk inches forward, every person's request requiring the receptionist to make multiple phone calls.

"You can believe what I said or not," I tell him. "It's up to you."

"I'm going to talk to Mr. Kingman about Riley Taylor," Hernandez says.

"I already did that," I reply. "He says he doesn't remember him. He has memory gaps."

"But he remembers you."

"He does."

"Especially after you say that little catchphrase."

I turn and look Hernandez straight in the eyes. Since we're the same height, I have a perfect view. His eyes are so dark that I can't see his pupils.

"Catchphrase?"

"It's in the notes," Hernandez says. "You said it at the station in Hollywood and when you were questioned on Lincoln Blvd. in Marina del Rey."

I know I can't play dumb any longer—it would make me look as if I really were a dunce.

"Oh," I say, as if just figuring out what he means. "You're talking about when I said 'four thousand bucks.'"

"What does it mean?" Hernandez asks.

"It's what Mr. Kingman is paying me to write his book."

"That's all you're making to write a book?"

"What I'm missing in compensation," I reply, "I'm making up in fun."

Hernandez's eyes close for a second, and I can see he's trying not to smile.

"So you say those words," he tells me, "to remind him who you are."

"It's like a private joke between us," I say.

It's finally our turn at the reception desk. The twenty-something receptionist finds Mr. Kingman's room number and calls the nurses's station. She listens for a moment, then looks up at us from her kneeling position on an ergonomic chair. I could use one of those with all the praying I've been doing lately.

"What is your relation to Mr. Kingman?" she asks in a weary, I-hate-my-job voice.

"I'm his employee," I say. "I need to speak with him about a work assignment."

"Family only," the receptionist says, unable to hide a smirk. Barring the door may be the only joy this woman gets from her job.

Before I can respond, the receptionist looks at Hernandez and says, "And you, sir?"

Hernandez reaches in his pocket and pulls out a black case, which he flips open to reveal his LAPD detective's badge.

"What is your business with Mr. Kingman?" she asks.

"That will have to remain between me and Mr. Kingman," he tells her and ekes out a subzero smile.

The receptionist glares at Hernandez, pushes aside an alien romance paperback—maybe I can write one of these when this gig is finished—and makes out a visitor's pass.

"Second floor," she says.

"Her too," Hernandez says, nodding his head toward me.

"Is this official business?" she asks.

"It is now," he says.

"Can you tell me if Mr. Kingman has had any other visitors?" I ask the receptionist.

"No," she says.

"He hasn't had any," I say, "or you can't tell me?"

"Next," she calls out, and a woman elbows me aside and launches into her request.

"Let's go," Hernandez says, nodding toward the elevator.

"I wonder if Mr. Kingman's son has been here," I say, thinking out loud.

"The son who reported you to the police for elder abuse?" Hernandez says.

"When that four thousand dollar check hit Mr. Kingman's bank account, his son was tipped off about it and filed the report without even trying to contact me."

"How's Kingman's relationship with his son?" Hernandez says as we take our places in the restless throng at the elevator.

"They don't get along," I say. "Definitely an adversarial relationship."

"Why's that?"

"For one thing, Mr. Kingman isn't his son's biological father. As Conrad grew older, he started to resent Mr. Kingman. After his mother died a few years ago, he was afraid he'd get disinherited. Mr. Kingman thinks Conrad is stealing from him and even asked me to report him to the police, which I refused to do."

The elevator finally arrives, but we can't fit inside. We wait for the next one.

"Do you think Conrad could have had anything to do with Riley Taylor's accident?" Hernandez asks.

"As far as I know," I say, "they don't, I mean, didn't know each other." I avoid looking at Hernandez and wonder if he'd noticed my slip into present tense.

"I have to explore all possibilities," Hernandez says, with no indication that he'd caught my verbal giveaway that Riley Taylor is still alive.

I have a sudden flash, wondering if I should tell Hernandez about Ryan, the detective that somebody hired to follow me. Since Ryan won't tell me who put him on my tail, maybe Hernandez can find out. I try to remember what I'd promised Ryan.

I go over it in my mind, recalling that Ryan broke into my apartment, confronted me about Milton's confidential file, said someone had paid him to steal it, but he hated the client who'd hired him, so offered to steal it back for me as soon as he got paid. He'd kept his word, and the file is now where I'd put it— in Pauline Granton's safe.

But I'd never promised to keep the transaction confidential—although my silence had been assumed. But what if Ryan's client had had something to do with Riley Taylor's car crash? Should I share these thoughts with Hernandez?

But Hernandez already seems to know I'm trying to decide whether or not to tell him something.

"Better spill it," he says as we step onto the elevator.

We're in the back, with people crammed in all the way to the front. For some reason, everyone is lined up in straight rows, as if we're a giant box of Q-Tips. I reach up and feel my hair—shorter than the tip of a Q-Tip—and wonder how long it will take the pixie to grow out.

"Still getting used to that new haircut," Hernandez remarks.

Hernandez seems to be keyed into my every move. I have enough experience with body language and subtle signs—voice tone, eye movements, head tilts—from untold hours of interviewing people that I can read him. And I imagine that he has as much experience or more interviewing people and he can read me. I feel so exposed in his presence—nowhere to hide, no way to conceal anything.

I'll try to give him bits and pieces so he has the impression he's getting the full story, but there's no way I can tell him that Riley Taylor is still alive. He'll have to figure that out himself, or Riley will have to turn himself in.

As we step off of the elevator, I hear a scary growl—and I think it's an editorial comment from a disgruntled visitor—but then realize I'm starving. I haven't eaten anything since the frozen waffles at Milton's house. When was that—eighteen hours ago?

"Should've finished your breakfast," Hernandez says.

"I wonder if this place has a lunchroom," I say.

"All hospitals do," he responds. "Do you want to grab something before we visit Kingman?"

"And wait for the elevator again? No thanks."

As we approach the nurses's station, I stand next to Hernandez and let him do the talking. After he explains why we're here and show our visitors' passes, the nurse—a doughy man in his twenties—directs us to a room halfway down the hall.

Two rooms from our destination, I stop and address Hernandez in a whisper.

"Let me go in first," I say. "Milton might get worried if he sees someone he doesn't know."

"I thought you called him Mr. Kingman."

"He likes me to call him Milton," I explain. "I think it makes him feel younger."

"Well, if you're ninety-one, I guess anything helps."

"Milton is ninety-one?"

"You missed that bit of research, huh?"

"He never mentioned his age. And, you're right, I never thought to check."

"How old did you think he was?"

"Around eighty," I say. "How did you find out? Does he still have a driver's license?"

"Gets it renewed every year."

I make my way toward Room 248. I just pray that Conrad isn't there. My stomach lets out another loud growl.

"Would you mind," I ask Hernandez, "getting me something from a snack machine while I share a few words alone with Mr. Kingman?"

"Dakota," he says, "I bought you a nice big breakfast and asked you to eat it. If you're hungry, there's nothing I can do about it. I have to be present during your entire conversation with Mr. Kingman."

"Can you at least let me walk in the door first?"

He moves aside and says, "Après vous."

When I give him a puzzled look, he replies, "My wife is a French teacher."

I step into the cool darkness of the room—thick drapes over the windows and heavy air conditioning blasting—and tiptoe toward Milton's hospital bed, where he's lying silent and still.

◀ THIRTY ▶

I stand next to Milton's hospital bed, listening for the sounds of his breathing and watching for the rise and fall of his chest—but hear and see nothing. I wonder why the nurse allowed us to see Milton without explaining his condition or prognosis.

Detective Hernandez stands behind me, holding a notebook and pencil—as if getting ready to take down Milton's last words.

I put my hand on Milton's wrist, trying to feel a pulse. I apply a bit more pressure and move my hand, searching for a sign of life. While trying to decide which saint or saints I can call on for assistance, Milton's eyes open wide, as if pulled by a string.

"Four thousand bucks," he says.

I let out an audible sigh and say, "I see your sense of humor is intact."

Milton's eyes graze the walls, and he asks, "What happened, Dakota? Where am I?"

"We were at the sheriff's station and you were having chest pains, so they brought you to the hospital."

"Did I have a heart attack?" he asks, moving his hands around his chest, as if trying to locate the reason for his hospital stay.

"I need to talk with your doctor," I say.

"I thought that's who he was," Milton says, motioning toward Hernandez.

Hernandez takes a step closer to the bed and says, "Mr. Kingman, I'm Detective Hernandez with LAPD."

"Did Conrad file another report against Dakota?"

"No, sir, he didn't."

"Then what do you want?"

"I'm investigating the circumstances surrounding the death of a writer named Riley Taylor."

"Oh," Milton says.

"Do you remember meeting Mr. Taylor?" Hernandez asks.

"Oh," Milton repeats.

"We're trying to speak with all of Mr. Taylor's acquaintances and business associates. Can you tell me about your meeting with Mr. Taylor."

"Why do you want to know about that?" Milton asks.

"Your conversation might shed some light on Mr. Taylor's concerns and interests at the time of his death."

"How did he die?"

"Car crash," Hernandez responds.

"Do you think his car was tampered with?"

"We're investigating a lot of different possibilities at the moment."

I try to jog Milton's memory, saying, "Remember when I asked if you'd met with Riley Taylor?"

"Yes," he says. "But I didn't feel like discussing it at the time."

"Why not?" I ask.

"I'm tired, Dakota," he says. "I'm so tired." He closes his eyes and takes a deep breath.

Hernandez looks at me and raises his eyebrows. Since the two of us can read each other so well, words aren't required. Hernandez is thinking we'd better prod Milton a bit more because this may be our last chance to get his statement.

"Milton," I say, just a touch above a whisper—and for all Milton's challenges of old age, his hearing is still good.

"Order me some breakfast," Milton says. "I haven't eaten anything since we had those frozen waffles yesterday afternoon."

▼

While waiting for a breakfast tray, I speak with the attending physician about Milton, and learn that he didn't have a heart attack. The doctor—a young woman named Vanessa Chen—explains that she's still awaiting test results and that Milton is scheduled for more tests today.

After she leaves the room, I ask Milton, "Did anyone call Conrad?"

"Conrad who?" Milton says.

"I think he should know you're in the hospital."

"If I tell him, it'll just cause me more stress. He'll be hovering over me, asking about my will."

I glance at Hernandez, and with a quick exchange of expressions we agree not to bring Conrad into the picture—at least for a while.

When Milton asks us to crank his bed into a sitting position, Hernandez does the honors.

"So where were we?" Milton says, but before we can answer adds, "When are they going to bring that tray?"

"They said thirty minutes forty-five minutes ago," I tell him.

"Don't you carry any snacks with you?" he asks.

"Those frozen waffles were the last thing I ate, too," I say. "If I had any snacks, I would have devoured them by now."

"I'm leaving," Milton says, sliding his feet over the side of the bed.

"No, please," I say. Then I remember something that might help.

I dig into my bag and find the almost-full package of Lorna Doone cookies—the ones I'd bought at the gas station the night I found out Riley Taylor wasn't dead. I keep my eyes down, afraid to catch Hernandez's look—fearing he'll see what I don't want to reveal.

"Here," I say, putting the Lorna Doones on the nightstand and pouring Milton a glass of water.

"Hand me one," he says.

After three cookies, Milton sighs as if his hunger panic has subsided. He drinks a full glass of water, then asks Hernandez to help him to the restroom.

When the breakfast tray finally arrives, Milton pushes it aside and eats more Lorna Doones.

"Mr. Kingman," Hernandez says, "I need to know what happened during your meeting with Riley Taylor."

"What do you want to know?"

"How did he learn you were looking for a ghostwriter?"

"I put an ad on Craigslist."

"You did that yourself?" Hernandez asks.

Milton shakes his head, saying, "I had help."

We wait a full minute for Milton to continue. I hand him the now-cold coffee from his breakfast tray, and he takes a few sips.

"I knew a publicist, a woman named Penelope Lauren, knew her from way back. I took her into my confidence, told her about the book I wanted to write. She put the ad on Craigslist and set up interviews for me at an office in Santa Monica."

"How can I get in touch with Ms. Lauren?" Hernandez asks.

"Sorry to say," Milton responds, "she passed away."

"When was that?" Hernandez asks.

"Right after I interviewed the ghostwriting candidates," Milton says. "Her death scared the hell out of me. I backed off from doing the project for another year."

"How did she die?" I ask.

"Penny was driving home from a premiere. She was shot to death at a stoplight in Beverly Hills."

"Oh, right," Hernandez says. "I remember that case. They never caught the shooter.

"And you think her murder might have something to do with what you revealed to her?" I ask.

"I can think of no other explanation," Milton says. "Every-one loved Penny."

"It couldn't have been a random event?" I ask.

"In Beverly Hills?" Milton says.

"In these meetings that Ms. Lauren set up for you, how many ghostwriters did you interview?" Hernandez asks.

"Had to be at least a dozen," Milton says. "This fellow Riley Taylor seemed the most capable and knowledgeable. I called him in for a second interview and showed him a folder of photographs and written material."

"What did the photographs depict?" Hernandez asked.

"Hasn't Dakota told you?" Milton says.

"No, sir, she hasn't," Hernandez responds.

Milton hesitates for a second and then, in interrogation parlance, spills it. It seems as if he's relieved to finally tell his outlandish tale to someone in authority. I get the impression that Milton hopes Hernandez will investigate, prove the truth of alien visitations, and release the story to the world.

After listening to Milton for about ten minutes, Hernandez says, "You're saying that you and Duke Galveston had meetings with aliens and these aliens told you how to manufacture a perpetual motion machine?"

"Among other things," Milton says.

"And what happened to the machine?"

"I wish I knew," Milton says. "When Duke moved to Vegas, it went with him. And who knows what happened to it there."

Hernandez glances my way, and I understand what he wants.

"Milton," I say, "I'm going to get some coffee. Do you want some?"

"I'll take a 7-Up," he says. "Now where was I?" He looks toward Hernandez. "Remind me."

"Mr. Kingman, I'll be right back. I have to phone the station and let them know where I am."

"Be right back," I say.

"Right-o," Milton says.

I walk to the end of the hall and sit in an alcove by a window. Hernandez pulls a package of Marlboros out of his pocket and sticks one in his mouth. He sees how I'm ogling the smokes and tosses the pack to me. I pull out a cigarette and hand him back the pack. We both stand there with unlit cigarettes in our hands. Hernandez sticks his between his lips and speaks with it in his mouth.

"So Mr. Kingman is suffering from dementia," he says.

"You hope so anyway," I say, taking a fake drag on my Marlboro, always a favorite brand.

"He's told you all this alien shit before?"

"That's what the book is about."

"Do you believe it?"

"The question is: Does he believe it?"

"Does he?"

"Absolutely."

"And he has photos of the aliens?" Hernandez asks. "That's what Riley Taylor was after?"

"I don't think Riley got more than a glance at those photos," I say. "That's why he was so determined to get his hands on them again."

"And you've seen these photos?" he says.

"I have."

"And . . ."

"I think it's hard to tell Hollywood from the real thing."

◀ THIRTY-ONE ▶

When we return to Milton's room a few minutes later, Dr. Chen is there—explaining about the tests Milton will take this afternoon.

As I approach Milton's bed, the doctor turns to me and says, "I really need a list of the medications that Mr. Kingman takes."

"Dakota," Milton says, "I told the lovely doctor that you'd go to my house and pick up my medicine. It's all on the kitchen counter."

"Okay," I say, "where did they put your keys?"

▼

I offer to drive myself to Milton's house—in my car, if it's still there, which is parked within walking distance—but Hernandez isn't about to get off the investigative merry-go-round with me as his prime person of interest.

As we pull out of the hospital parking lot, I spot a black SUV at the curb—and, though I can't read the plate, I'm pretty sure the vehicle belongs to Riley Taylor. After he figured out which hotel we were at when I phoned him, he probably went there, asked around, and found someone who overheard us talking about going to the hospital.

From the corner of my eye, I see his car pull out of its parking space. I figure the vehicle is right behind us—and try not to give anything away to the ever-vigilant Detective Hernandez.

As we head toward Milton's place, the question that goes through my mind is: Who's smarter—Riley or Hernandez? I'd say it's an even match. Riley is too smart to get caught tailing Hernandez, and Hernandez is too smart not to notice someone following him.

I check my phone and see that it's after one o'clock, twenty-four hours since I've had a real meal—my lunch yesterday with Shelly Morris. I know if I don't eat soon I'll pass out. I'm surprised I don't have a migraine.

Before I can voice my request, Hernandez, makes a left onto a side street and parks next to the Siam Thai restaurant—my favorite cuisine, especially when I'm starving.

It's lunchtime, so the place is crowded. Hernandez explains that we're in a hurry and asks the young Thai waiter if he'll please find a place for us. Soon, a table has been cleared and we're studying the ten-page menu. I feel like ordering everything on it, but decide I'd better not overdo it, and opt for my standard Pad Thai and vegetable rolls. Hernandez orders green curry.

While we wait for the food, the last thing I want to do is subject myself to Hernandez's penetrating stare. I excuse myself and head for the restroom. It's a nice, clean spot with thick paper towels and liquid soap. I lock the door, take off my blouse and give myself a quick sponge bath. When I look in the mirror, I don't recognize myself. My hair is sticking up all over the place and yesterday's eye makeup is nowhere near my eyes.

I wet my hair, slick it down, wash my face, apply eyeliner and lipstick, put on my blouse, take a deep breath and feel like a whole new person—not one who's had little sleep or food for the past day.

As I make my way back to the table, I see a man sitting in my spot with his back to me. I'd recognize that bald head anywhere.

When I get to the table, the man stands and turns to me.

"I'm sorry I put you through this, Dakota," Riley Taylor says.

"Both of you," Hernandez barks, "sit down."

But before I can obey the command, Riley puts his arms around me and keeps them there for what feels like a long time.

I whisper in his ear, "It's okay."

The waiter appears with our order, and I slide into the white booth—Riley taking a place next to me. The waiter asks if we intend to share the food or if Riley wants to order something.

"We won't be here long," Hernandez says, not answering the question, but the waiter is too polite to ask anything else. He smiles, nods, and glides away.

My appetite is gone. Someone would have to force me to eat even one noodle in my Pad Thai. But I'm afraid if I don't try to at least take a few bites, I'll be in serious trouble. It's been years since I've missed a meal—let alone a whole day's worth.

I stare at my plate, not wanting to look at Hernandez, who I know is mad as hell that I didn't tell him Riley was still alive—and I don't want to look at Riley because I'll burst into tears if I get another glimpse of his guilt-stricken face.

Nobody's talking. It feels as if we're all trying to figure out what the others are thinking—in effect, attempting to read minds—something that as detective, ghostwriter, and journalist we all think we're good at. Anyway, how can words ever express so many complex thoughts and emotions?

"What the f**k?" Hernandez finally says.

I feel a lecture coming—the one about the amount of LAPD manpower wasted investigating Riley Taylor's "death under mysterious circumstances." Hernandez starts to speak, but his words get jumbled on the way out and he sputters to a stop. There are so many things he wants to say—and they're all tumbling from his lips at once.

He stands, glares at us, says, "Stay here," and heads for the front door. He stands on the sidewalk outside the restaurant, lights a Marlboro, takes a deep drag, then dials his cell phone.

Riley puts his right hand over my left hand, which is resting on the seat between us.

"Your hair looks good," he says, drawing the intended smile from me.

"Great barber," I say, "but I can't recommend him."

"And why's that?"

"Too expensive."

"What happened last night?" he asks. "I phoned you over and over."

I avoid looking at Riley in case Hernandez is watching us—which he probably is. If eagle-eyed Hernandez sees Riley and me looking chummy and staring into each other's eyes, he may start to think I had something to do with killing the man driving Riley's car when it exploded.

After I offer Riley the broad outlines of my night at the L.A. County Sheriff's station in Marina del Rey and my morning at the hospital with Milton and Hernandez, he again apologizes for getting me mixed up in his trouble. I know he's sincere about his remorse—and that he understands I'm in serious shit for withholding evidence and could get arrested as an accomplice, or at the least for aiding and abetting.

"Don't worry," he says. "I'll make sure they understand you had nothing to do with anything. "

"Just tell them what happened," I say. "Just tell the truth about everything."

Boom, he's back. Hernandez slides into the other side of the booth.

"Okay, here's the plan," Hernandez says. "Dakota, you go to Kingman's house, pick up his medicine, bring it to the hospital, and stay there. That's it, no other stops."

He stares ice-pick eyes at Riley, but the resurrected journalist doesn't lift his glance from the tabletop.

"Look at me," Hernandez says.

Riley takes his time raising his gaze toward Hernandez.

"Miss Graph is waiting," the detective says. "First name…"

"Poly . . . " Riley and I say at once.

"Heard that one before, huh?" Hernandez says.

"Maybe you should hire Dakota," Riley says, "to write you some new material."

▼

Hernandez insists on giving me a lift to my car, parked a few blocks away near Lincoln and Maxella. After ushering Riley into the back seat, he nods for me to sit upfront. I'm carrying the Thai food in a takeout bag and right away the smell permeates Hernandez's pristine Honda. Oh, how that fish sauce can stink up the joint. I roll down the window and hope some outside air will help. It seems to take less than a minute for

Hernandez to reach my car, still parked where I'd left it facing north on Lincoln.

"Remember what I told you," Hernandez says as he pulls to the curb.

"Okay," I respond, opening the door.

"What did I tell you?"

"She said 'okay,'" Riley pipes in from the back.

"I want to hear her say it."

"You want me to go to Mr. Kingman's house, pick up his medicine, go back to the hospital, and stay there."

"What else?"

"Make no other stops."

"Here," Hernandez says, handing me a business card. "If anything, and I mean anything, comes up to prevent you from doing just as I've instructed, call me right away. Until this gets cleared up, you're in a shitload of trouble. So just do as I say, and I'll put in a good word for you with the judge."

"That's not funny," Riley says.

"Right," Hernandez responds, "I'm gonna hire Dakota to write me some new material."

As I start to get out of the car, I feel Riley give me a light touch on the shoulder—sort of a bon voyage gesture. I want to turn around and look at him, but figure it's best to just keep staring straight ahead.

Before I close the door, Hernandez says, "I'll call you in Kingman's hospital room in ninety minutes. That should give you plenty of time to drive to Brentwood and back."

"In rush hour?"

"Two hours tops," he says.

I ease the door shut, but Hernandez pushes it open and shoves the bag of Thai food at me.

"And take your stinking lunch with you," he says.

As soon as I slam the car door, Hernandez guns it out of there. Riley looks out the back window, but I can't read his expression, his face hazy behind the Los Angeles dust and grime.

While I wait for the light to change so I can cross the street, I feel my legs wobble. I have to put one hand on the lamppost to keep from falling over. I see a Starbucks sign like a green life raft on the other side of the street. I'm sweating and my heart is thumping at double speed. My face is flushed. I need to sit down, someplace cool, someplace where I can eat something. Crossing the street, I feel as if I'm swimming—the air feels like muddy water that I have to push through.

When I reach the curb, I start to throw the Thai food into a trash bin, but stop myself. As sick as I feel, as tired as I am, and as inconvenient as it is to carry the stinkin' bag, I can't toss my uneaten lunch—too much Catholic guilt.

After buying a bagful of drinks at Starbucks—a bottle of water, an iced tea, and a cup of coffee—plus two scones, I make it back to my car, which feels as hot as the inside of a coffee pot, but doesn't smell as good—especially now that the Thai food is in the back.

I open all the windows and sit there sipping iced tea and fanning myself with the parking ticket that I just removed from the windshield. When I've cooled off a bit, I take slow nibbles of the scone—nowhere near as good as the one Riley bought for yesterday's breakfast.

As I try to get the food into my stomach, I let my mind go blank. My head hurts—not a headache, just brain overload. I want to zone out for a while. It feels good not to think, not to worry. I feel myself calming down, but then hear a raucous voice scream, "Dakota! Dakota! Dakota!"

I turn and see Joyce stumbling down the block in her white wedgies. My first thought is: how in the hell did she get all the way over here? And my next thought: Well, at least I know what to do with the Thai food.

As soon as she opens the car door, Joyce holds her nose and says, "Who died in here?"

"Would you be interested in some Pad Thai?"

"And why would I want your leftovers?"

"I didn't touch it."

"And you're gonna drive around in a hot car with this stink bomb? Why didn't you just throw it away?"

When I don't respond, Joyce leans over the back seat, grabs the bag from the floor, then darts out the door and dumps my lunch in the trash bin. I watch her making a big display of dusting off her hands as she heads back to the car.

"Let's go," Joyce says.

But before I can answer, she taps her forehead and says, "Finally." She digs in her rolling duffle bag and pulls out two plain white boxes. She hands one to me and puts the other on her lap.

"I've been carrying these around for days," she says. "Go ahead, open it."

"Joyce," I say, "I don't have time to explain, but I'm in a hurry."

"You're always in a hurry," she says.

"I have a life-or-death reason for not driving you back to Los Feliz," I say.

"You gotta drive me back," she responds. "I can't walk another step in these effing torture devices."

"I can drop you at Sunset," I tell her. "That's as far as I'm going."

"Open your present," she says.

I slide the lid from the six-inch square box and pull out a small fan.

Joyce opens her box and takes out another fan.

"I already put batteries mine," she tells me. "Yours runs on the cigarette lighter."

She holds up her fan and says, "Ready, set, go."

I plug the fan into the lighter, and we flip the switch at the same time. We have liftoff—or at least a hint of air circulation. I fit the fan into the accompanying suction cup and stick it on the dashboard in front of me. In this heat and in my current state of exhaustion, the fan is a godsend.

"Thank you," I say, knowing that Joyce will try to extract a favor from me as payback for her largesse. I just hope I can send her on her way before she asks for something major.

212

"Who cut your hair?" Joyce asks.

"A friend."

"Freebie?"

"Oh there were costs attached," I reply.

"Is that where you've been for the last two days and nights?"

I decide to direct the conversation to Joyce's favorite topic —Joyce—asking how she's been and what she's doing on the Westside. And, my oh my, does she have some exciting news to report—her first art show, at a gallery a couple of blocks away in Venice.

As she relates the details, I tune out because I've just remembered something I need to take care of right away —the DNA samples. I have to mail them today.

I make a right on Wilshire and head up a few blocks, pulling into a parking space down the street from Santa Monica's Will Rogers Post Office Branch.

"I thought you were dropping me at Sunset," Joyce moans.

"I need to make a quick stop," I tell her.

I pull Hernandez's business card from my pocket, grab my cell, and dial the number. But after two rings, the phone goes dead. I flip open the car's middle console, hoping the charger is there—but no.

"Do you want to wait here or go inside?" I ask.

"Inside where?"

After I explain, she says, "I'll wait here, but while you're in there, get me some stamps. I'm sending out postcards for my opening."

When I return twenty minutes later, Joyce is standing outside the car smoking. For once, the sight of a cigarette doesn't fill me with longing. Maybe I'm over the hump—or maybe I'm just too tired and hungry and queasy to desire a nicotine rush.

After we get in the car, I hand Joyce a sheet of postcard stamps and she rummages in her bag and pulls out a twenty-dollar bill.

"Keep the change," she says, ever the master of the grand gesture. I know the big request is coming soon.

When I put the key in the ignition, Joyce says, "Wait."

"I am really in a hurry, Joyce," I tell her.

"I'm gonna take the Wilshire bus," she says, opening the car door.

"Okay. Well, thanks for the fan," I say, turning it on.

She looks over at me and says, "Dakota, you've always been a good friend."

Uh oh, here it comes. I've got to get out of here now.

"Thanks, Joyce. Now I really have to go."

"I'd do anything for you," she says. "And I hope you'd do the same for me."

Oh, my God. It's got to be something big, something I would never, ever agree to.

". . . and I have no one else to turn to . . ."

"Joyce, please," I say, "I am in a lot of trouble right now. I can't get into details. But it's serious, really, really serious. Please, please whatever it is, let's discuss it later."

"It can't be later," she says. "It has to be now."

And so she asks. And I was right—it is the last thing I want to do. Defying the few rational cells still firing in my brain, I reach in my bag and hand Joyce the key to my apartment.

◀ THIRTY-TWO ▶

Out of habit, I park a block away from Milton's place—not that there's any danger of my hospitalized client spotting the bucket of bolts I drive. For that matter, he's already enjoyed an extended excursion along the California coast in my car—and never mentioned its advanced age or lack of air conditioning.

As I walk down this Brentwood sidewalk on this August afternoon, it feels like a long, long time since I started working on Milton Kingman's book—so much has happened during the past week. I have to stop and remember what day it is. I think it's Friday—a week after I accepted the assignment.

At Milton's front door, I fumble in my bag—and for a panicky minute think I might have given his key to Joyce. I rummage around, but can't find the key. I wonder what time it is and if I've already missed the deadline Hernandez gave me. Two hours couldn't have gone by, could they?

Now what? I need to bring Milton's meds to the hospital. Should I see if he left a window open? No, too risky. I'm not ready for another police interrogation—three times is more than enough for one week.

I stop, take a long, deep breath, and direct my attention to St, Anthony, reverting to my childhood version of the prayer for finding lost things: *Tony, Tony, look around. Something's lost and must be found.* I repeat the incantation a few times and then pat my back pocket and feel the outline of a key—or else a cat treat I forgot about.

After a bit of silent communion with Tony to thank him for the help, I slide the key in the lock. As I'm about to turn it, I glance to my right and see the front door at the next house open a few inches. The voice of an elderly woman wisps toward me like thread of smoke.

"Who are you?" she says.

"I work for Mr. Kingman."

"No you don't."

"I'm writing a book for him."

"He didn't come home last night."

"Mr. Kingman is in the hospital undergoing some tests," I explain. "His doctor sent me here to pick up his medicine."

The door slams—expressing in volume what the woman's faint voice can't communicate.

I've got to get out of here before the Brentwood cops show up and arrest me for breaking and entering. Who knows, maybe they'll try to nail me for kidnapping, too.

When I push open the door, it seems to let out a short squeal—like when a woman screams in a horror movie and covers her mouth to stop the noise. I step into the house and shove Milton's key into my back pocket.

The scent of lemon oil tempts me to take a quick tour of the rooms to view Milton's collection of midcentury furniture and lamps—"only for five minutes." But I know myself—how I lose track of time and a few minutes turns into an hour or more.

I head for the kitchen and its heavenly aquamarine-colored appliances. The whole house is spotless, as if someone had just cleaned it from one end to the other. When I search the kitchen counter, Milton's medicine isn't there. After a quick check of the bathroom and Milton's bedroom, I figure it's best to call and ask.

As I pick up the phone in the living room, I hear a key turn in the front door lock. Before I get a chance to dial the hospital, the door opens and Conrad and his Great Dane rumble into the house. At first, Conrad doesn't notice me, perhaps mistaking my stock-still body for a statue or a hat rack. But after a second, Rudy is in front of me—emitting a grumble that sounds like, "Get out."

Conrad turns to me and squints, as if trying to read a newspaper without his glasses. When he registers who I am—perhaps thinking he was encountering Milton's housecleaner—he lets out something that sounds like a cross between a cough and a laugh, but comes across as a bark. Man and beast have changed places—Rudy is talking and Conrad is woofing. And I am dog meat.

"Let me explain," I say.

"Where's my father?" Conrad says, taking a step toward me. "What have you done to him?"

Rudy sits up and snarls as Conrad lurches toward me. I throw down the phone and back away, trying not to run into any of the vintage furniture.

"Your father's in the hospital. He was having chest pains. They're doing tests. The doctor sent me here to pick up his medicine."

By this time, I've backed all the way to the kitchen. Conrad and Rudy follow me into the room. I think I've explained my presence, until Conrad reaches into a kitchen drawer and pulls out a snubnosed revolver. At first, I think this is a joke—that the gun is a movie prop—but as he gets closer I can see it's real.

How do I handle this situation? Do I try to reason? Act placating? Apologetic? Do I act tough? Unafraid? Laugh in his face?

"Please, Conrad, put down the gun," I say, figuring it's best to appear sincere and get to the point.

"Oh how I love the Stand Your Ground laws," he says, baring his teeth in a creepy laugh.

"This is not your house," I say. "Besides, I'm unarmed and not threatening you."

"You know it all, don't you, smartass?" he snarls, hot spit shooting from the sides of his mouth.

"Conrad, please calm down," I say, sidling toward the back door.

"You've been causing trouble since you showed up—telling my dad to report me to the police, saying I was stealing from him."

"I swear that never happened."

I reach for the doorknob, but Conrad lunges toward me, knocking away my hand. I grab his right forearm and we struggle back and forth—he's so tall that he has to hunch down to keep track of me because I keep ducking and darting out of his field of vision.

I can hear Rudy grumbling, "Get out," but he doesn't join in the scuffle—I figure he's probably waiting for a command from his master.

For all his height and heft, Conrad isn't very strong—he's like a big, tall, hollow saguaro cactus: bristle and bluster but without much real bite. His chest is heaving, and he's sweating and trying to catch his breath from the exertion. I thought I was in bad shape—but compared to him I'm a sleek bobcat.

The gun goes off, the force sending us both backwards. My ears are ringing and there's a smell of sulfur—making me wonder just which level of the inferno I've fallen to. Rudy is yelping and Conrad has his hands over his ears—I hope the bullet didn't strike either of them, but can't stop to find out because something more interesting has grabbed my attention: The revolver at my feet.

I pick up the gun and hold it at my side. "Are you hurt?" I ask.

"What the hell do you care?" Conrad whines, then lowers his bulk onto one of Milton's delicate teakwood chairs. "You're doing your best to destroy me—turning my dad against me, having him shut me out of his will, saying I'm a criminal, trying to get me arrested."

"Think what you like, Conrad," I tell him. "Nothing I say is going to change your mind. I've got to get back to the hospital."

"Which hospital?" he asks, his head in his hands.

I don't answer, pretending not to hear him as I look around for the bullet hole, but can't find it—guess I'll have to leave that for the forensics team.

"Where's my father?"

"Conrad," I say, opening and closing the kitchen drawers, "your father will call when he's ready to see you."

"He won't want to see me."

"I'll make sure he calls. Give me your phone number," I say, handing him a tablet and pencil.

In one of the drawers I find a small black case—and unzip it to reveal bottles of prescription medications. I grab my bag, stuff the case inside, and pick up the piece of paper with Conrad's phone number.

"How do I know you're not holding my father for ransom?" he asks.

"If you're worried, feel free to contact LAPD," I reply. "Ask for Detective Hernandez. He knows where your father is."

When I head toward the front door. Rudy follows along— and I turn to see if the dog is okay. He gazes up at me with a look of what appears to be glee—happy, I guess, that someone has bested the nutcase he has to live with. I feel sorry for the poor pooch, and give him a couple of pats with my left hand— since I'm still holding the gun in my right.

"I want my swabs back," Conrad yells after me.

"Too late," I say. "Already mailed in the tests."

"How long for the results?"

"Two weeks."

" I don't want to know," he says.

"It's the only chance you have at a piece of Duke Galveston's fortune," I say. "Or to spend time with the man who may be your biological father."

"And who would that be?"

"I promised the man's wife I wouldn't say anything until we got the DNA results. If it's a positive match, she's agreed to allow you to see him."

"Agreed to allow me to see him?" Conrad repeats. "Don't tell me he's . . ."

"Yes," I say.

"Then what would be the point?"

"For starters, how about closure?" I tell him.

Before walking out the door, I slide the revolver into the side pocket of my bag. For some reason, I don't want to leave it in the house—concerned that Conrad and a gun are not a good mix. I've never handled a weapon in my life and don't want to start, but I see no other choice but to bring it with me.

When I get in my car, I remember to take the revolver out of my bag and put it in the glove compartment. I have no idea how to unload the gun—and figure if I try, it might go off again.

Turning onto Sunset, I check the time on my dashboard clock—it's four thirty-eight. I think I was supposed to show up at the hospital around four. I've got to find a payphone and call Hernandez. But where in this part of town? My only real chance is to stop at a gas station and ask if I can use someone's cell.

As I make my way to Lincoln Blvd., I see a black SUV behind me. For a moment, I think it's Riley, but it can't be. Hernandez wouldn't have let him go this fast. I know I've seen that car before—but with the dark tinted windows, it's impossible to look inside. I have a hunch who's shadowing me.

I drive for a few blocks, then pull into a parking space. The SUV glides in behind me. I get out of my car, approach the vehicle and knock on the window. I wait for thirty seconds, then knock again. The window on the passenger's side lowers bit by slow bit, sounding like it's saying "huh" on the way down.

When I duck down and peek through the opening, I see my gut instinct was correct. The pieces fall into place, and I realize who hired Ryan to follow me.

◀ THIRTY-THREE ▶

Seven weeks later, in early October, I drive to Santa Monica, where Milton now lives in an oceanfront retirement home. It's a luxurious setting—with plush furnishings, gourmet meals, and enjoyable activities for the residents.

Milton has a studio apartment with his own bathroom and other amenities. I've visited him a few times since he moved in a few weeks ago, and he seems to be enjoying his new surroundings. I think he even has his eye on a few of the ladies.

Today is the big day—when I hand over Milton's completed book, entitled *King B: When B-Movies Reigned in Hollywood.* As I wait in the lobby for Milton to join me, I have never felt more relieved at finishing a ghostwriting project.

I had to break it to Milton in slow steps that the whole alien visitation business was a practical joke that Duke Galveston had played on him. He wasn't convinced until Shelly Morris stopped by the hospital and revealed that Duke had sworn her to secrecy about how he'd tricked him.

"But why?" Milton had asked Shelly.

"Because he could," Shelly told him, taking his hand and holding it. "Because he enjoyed making fools out of other people."

I wasn't sure it was right to strip away Milton's illusions about his former business partner. I wondered if Milton might be too old for such a stark and hurtful realization. But to do his book justice, I had to find out the truth—and help him face it.

When the DNA results came in, I wasn't surprised to learn that Conrad's biological father is Albert Sims—Pauline Granton's husband—who'd turned his back on Geraldine when she told him she was pregnant, because he didn't trust she was carrying his child. But some part of him must have always known she'd given birth to his son—though he'd suppressed the fact from both himself and his wife.

Conrad has visited Albert many times and has even found his long-lost father lucid on a few occasions. He's formed a closer bond with Pauline Granton, who has welcomed him as a son. She's even opened up her house to Rudy, and the dog—who seems partial to females—adores her.

Pauline asked Shelly Morris to stay on and "help manage"—offering the homeless woman a home without appearing to do so. Shelly's presence in the household has made a marked difference in Pauline's outlook—leaving her feeling less isolated and alone. The two old friends find solace in each other's company as life continues to revolve around Albert and his struggle with the world's worst affliction.

Milton took the news of Conrad's paternity with good grace—relieved, I think, that Duke Galveston wasn't the sire. Milton and Conrad have established a truce of sorts—with Milton leaving his stepson well provided for—and enjoy regular visits and phone calls.

For the past few weeks, I've shared my apartment with Joyce as she prepares for her first gallery show. She was discovered while selling her drawings at Hollywood and Highland—and after this exhibit may have enough money to buy a condo. Now wouldn't that be a happy ending?

As for Riley Taylor, he failed his lie detector test—and the police have him locked up while they investigate the explosion that killed the man driving his car. I don't believe Riley had anything to do with the man's death—but feel he's withholding information for some reason. When and if he gets out of jail, we'll see where things lead.

My cats were happy when I stopped chasing the story for Milton's book and sat down and started to write the tale of the 1950s B-Movie King and his partnership with Duke Galveston.

I think Marelle was glad when I resumed my cat caring duties—because her free time is now limited. She's not only working as a psychic in Ryan's detective agency—but she's also dating the detective.

Who hired Ryan to follow me and steal Milton's confidential file? Was it Conrad? Riley? Shelly? Pauline? No, no, no, and no. It was Milton himself, who wanted to make sure he could trust me. For years, his life had been run by fear—fear of shadowy figures, fear of his story getting out, fear of repercussions—until he didn't trust anyone anymore. He had to be sure I wasn't a spy, a turncoat, or an opportunist.

As I wait for Milton, the urge to close my eyes and sleep comes over me. I feel as if I'm on a river, drifting far, far away from work and cares and worries. I let myself float along for a while, but then turn the boat around and head back to shore.

I force my eyes open and see a caregiver wheeling Milton toward me. As my employer gets closer, I say our old refrain one last time, "Four thousand bucks."

He smiles, reaches in his pocket, pulls out an envelope, and hands it to me.

As I look inside, he says, "Make that six thousand bucks."

I finished the book under the deadline, and he remembered to pay the bonus. Not to brag, but I feel I've earned every cent of it.

THE END

www.ingramcontent.com/pod-product-compliance
Lightning Source LLC
Chambersburg PA
CBHW060141130626
46556CB00006B/2445